LEMONS

LEMONS

Kasia Jaronczyk

Mansfield Press

Copyright © Kasia Jaronczyk 2017
All Rights Reserved
Printed in Canada

Library and Archives Canada Cataloguing in Publication

Jaronczyk, Kasia, author
    Lemons / Kasia Jaronczyk.

Short stories.
ISBN 978-1-77126-140-1 (softcover)

    I. Title.

PS8619.A76L46 2017   C813'.6   C2017-902141-9

Cover Image: Cezary Jaronczyk
Editor: Julie Booker
Design: Denis De Klerck

The publication of *Lemons* has been generously supported by the Canada Council for the Arts and the Ontario Arts Council.

Mansfield Press Inc.
25 Mansfield Avenue, Toronto, Ontario, Canada M6J 2A9
Publisher: Denis De Klerck
www.mansfieldpress.net

To all my loved ones.

TABLE OF CONTENTS

GIRLS

Lemons / 11
The Pet / 19
Diament Girls / 27
Epidemic (Director's Cut) / 35
Portrait / 51
Bozia / 63

WOMEN

Cicada / 75
Glaucoma / 87
The Rug / 99
Muse / 111
Bypass / 119

GIRLS

LEMONS

Julita looks at me with her eyes crinkling in the sunlight and says, swear on the Mother of God you won't tell anyone, or my father will kill me. We are sitting on a pile of crumbling bricks at the edge of the construction site that will become my school's swimming pool. The smell of wet cement and drywall dust in the wind.

I had a baby, she whispers. Her lips tickle my ear. I had to give it away.

Who's the father?

She has a new father now, she says, and picks at the milky-pink paint peeling off the carpet beater stand rising in front of us like bars of a cage. On the other end Gosia is doing chin-ups. She is tiny and skinny, but very strong—she can do ten chin-ups, while I can only do two or three. She lives across the hallway. Her father is a policeman. He likes to smoke on the balcony in an undershirt, tight round his bulging stomach and floppy breasts. He beats Gosia because she's deaf. It must hurt a lot because he has enormous arms.

I wonder about having two dads. They will both spank the baby when it grows up. I giggle.

I'm not allowed to tell who he is, Julita says, and stares at the apartment block in front of us, the bare patch of grass under my bedroom window and the tangled greenery of her dad's illegal garden on city property.

I want to ask her what it was like to make a baby, but I'm too shy. Everybody knows Julita's secret; many girls say she lies, but it still feels nice to be singled out today. My best friend Natalia asked her mother if it hurts to have a man's dick in your pussy. I wouldn't dare. But I think Natalia's mom was lying when she said it feels pleasant. Maybe it doesn't hurt, but it cannot feel nice.

I look at Julita's mud-puddle eyes, her short flat nose and crooked bangs, and I don't think I believe her. I see her large, dark nipples, round and symmetrical through the fabric of her shirt, and I remember her thick pubic hair when we peed behind a discarded sheet of drywall. I change my mind. I lean closer. I can feel the hair on her calves brush against mine. Tell me more, I keep thinking. Her side presses against my ribs briefly, her damp breath scalds my neck, she's about to say something, I know it, and then her father calls her name. She springs away from me as if I'd pushed her and scampers towards our apartment building. I stumble to catch up with her—she's fourteen and I'm only eleven, but we are in the same grade.

From the sidewalk around our apartment block I can see the buxom inky mermaid on Julita's father's arm through a lilac bush drooping with swollen bunches of flowers. His hairy hand is grasping a pair of shears with which he clips the branches that stick out. Lilacs always make me think of the Donkey Skin Princess whose stepfather wants to marry her because she looks so much like her mother. The fairy godmother, whose appearance is heralded by the smell of lilacs, advises the princess to make unreasonable demands to prevent the wedding: a dress the colour of the sun, then the colour of the moon and so on, and then the hide of the king's magic donkey that spits out gold coins. But the king always grants her wishes. Finally, the princess has to flee, dressed in the donkey skin like a beggar. Julita's large breasts jiggle under her blouse. I've seen her mother wear it. I am still waiting for my breasts to grow. I touch my nipples every night to check. Urszula, who lives above us, has breasts shaped like cups of aspic. She smokes with boys in a corner of the schoolyard, behind the scaffolding against an unfinished wall. Every evening Urszula's father hollers out his window, Get home this instant. The boys grab and straddle her, and she screams and laughs. Mama told me girls are supposed to have self-respect. That's why I'm always alone. Urszula's father beats her because she loves these boys more than him. She says that her father gets very sweaty when he spanks her, and after he's done he washes his hands and has a can of beer. You're just like your mother, he yells. I look nothing like her, Urszula tells us.

Julita has five younger sisters and she makes dinners for them because her mother slumps in a foldable chair in the garden all day, empty *Żywiec* bottles around her like a fence. When she goes inside, she holds onto the wall. Julita's father disappears for weeks, and when he returns, he has new tattoos. Mermaids and anchors. He's like a pirate. Gold teeth shine in the corners of his mouth. No parrot, but he keeps a pigeon under an empty crate in his garden. Its foot is tied to one of the slats with a piece of string.

Tata also leaves sometimes. He travels to England or America, I don't exactly know where, but they speak English there. I miss him. At night he massages my neck and feet when I have migraines. Mama tells us that we'll follow him, but it hasn't happened yet. I stopped telling my friends that I'll become *Indianka* and live in a teepee, because he always returns. And I am always disappointed, in spite of the chewing gum, jeans and Barbies he brings. He came back last week and ogled me like the men who smoke at the back of the grocery where I buy potatoes. I told Mama about it, but she said I was imagining things.

A few days later my brother Tomek and I were drawing in our bedroom when the front door slammed. Tata was back from work. He called us over. What's this? He kicked our shoes scattered in the hallway. He grabbed our jackets and school bags and threw them at us. Don't you know what hangers are for? Go lie down on the bed, he shouted and stomped to his bedroom. He'd been telling us to keep our stuff tidy for days. Why get angry today? On the door of his wardrobe is a long metal rail on which hang his ties and belts. I pressed my head into the mattress. The pain was sharp and left a sting that lingered like a stench. At dinner Mama asked him how was his day. He said he didn't want to talk about it. Back to normal.

We talk about our dads with our friends. Our dads spank us. This is what they do. They hit us and sometimes they take us to the movies or to fairs and amusement parks. Mothers do shopping, peel potatoes and cook all day. Fathers work. Our mothers stand gossiping in front of the apartment building, their shopping bags and arms tethering them to the ground like tents until our fathers send us to bring them home. Our dads are hungry. We show off our dads. Whose dad hits the hardest, most often, most fairly. Whose father is the best. We play a game. Say beef. Beef. Your dad is a thief. Say duck. Duck. Your dad is a lazy fuck. Say sick. Your dad has a tiny prick. Say nerve, your dad is a perv. Say lemon, your dad is a felon.

Natalia's father doesn't beat her because he's an artist— an artist is a different kind of man. He's an opera singer and he doesn't scream because he is saving his voice. To punish her he stops talking. They lived in America for a while, and Natalia brought back Barbies and a baby doll that cries real tears and sucks bottles and pacifiers. Natalia is in love with Tomek, and I with his best friend Michał. Michał and my brother play video games at a small café in the Hollow, in the basement of an apartment building where our street dips down a little hill. Tomek begs Mama for change, but he gives it all to Michał who hogs the video games.

I play "Statues" with Michał, my brother, and Natalia. My brother and Michał stand still in front of the two steel poles under the green glass awning of our apartment building. I say, Oh, look at this beautiful statue and I lean my back against Michał; Natalia does the same to my brother. Then the statues come to life—Michał grabs me hard and I jump and scream. His large hands have dark crescents of dirt behind the fingernails and leave red prints on my arms. I am floating and sinking when he holds me. I can feel the pressure of each of his fingers down to my bones, his breath on my neck, his chest pressing against my shoulder blades. I want him to clutch me over and over again. Natalia tells me she feels the same when my brother grabs her. That is weird, because when he touches me I hardly notice it unless it hurts.

We also play teeter-totter on the two-wheeled wagon, which belongs to Michał's father. It's the only thing parked in the lot. The playground, built of dark wood planks behind the garbage shed, is wrecked, burned by gangs of teenage boys that Urszula follows around. The wagon teeter-totters on the asphalt, and bumps us up in the air, Michał's father screams at us from the balcony to stop or he'll come down and give us a beating. I don't know why he cares so much—he has no car to pull the wagon with. I don't know anyone who has a car. We all walk or take a bus.

One day on an overcrowded bus my parents and I get separated. I'm surrounded by strangers, grasping a stirrup-like holder, cradling my cheek on the inside of my raised arm. An old man is staring at me like he knows me or wants to ask me something. His eyes have an unfocused, glazed look. His hands are large and hairy. I shoot him a disgusted glare. My parents emerge from the crowd and start talking to him. I know him—Michał's father. I didn't recognize him without his glasses.

The next day, in the parking lot, I want to tell Natalia what happened and how weird it was, but she has something more important to say—she has run up to me and is out of breath. She was walking from the mailbox to bring a letter to her father—she waves it in front of my face—when a furry hand came out from the shadow where the stairs lead to the basement, and grazed her ankle. And a man said, do you want me to lick your little lemon?

What did you do? I ask. I hate lemons. They burn your tongue like the nettles that grow in the rubble on construction sites and sting my thighs when I get too close.

I ran, says Natalia and laughs, I thought his hand was a cat. It was so large and bristly, and moved so fast.

Who was he?

I couldn't see his face.

He had a beard? I ask

No...I don't know... It was too dark.

Why would he want lemons? I ask. We should give him some. Do you have any at your place?

No, she says. Do you?

No—only at Christmas or for a name-day party.

We go to my apartment anyway. Mama is out shopping, so I ask my dad, who's sitting on the couch reading a paper and eating a hard-boiled egg.

We don't have any lemons, he says from behind the pages.

Hi Mr. Kowalczyk, Natalia says.

Hi, Magda, he says.

It's Natalia, dad. I look at her and roll my eyes.

Magda is not my friend. She stole Dominika from me. Now they sit together behind me and talk in class, while I have to share my desk with Rafał who is fat and has no friends. Magda's father beats her when she gets bad marks. She says he uses a wide belt with an oval shaped clasp with a picture of the White Eagle. He beats her often because she's stupid. She's been held back in her grade like my cousin Stasia.

It's hard to keep track of all you kids, my dad says, and wipes the yellow crumbs of yolk from his fingers on his thighs.

There is a man in the stairwell of Natalia's building who wanted to eat a lemon, I say.

No, Natalia giggles, and tells him what he really said.

Tata gets up quickly. Show me where he is. He grabs his jacket and we run outside.

The man is gone.

Tata drops us off at Natalia's place. We watch from the balcony. Tata, Natalia's dad, and a few other fathers go in and out of apartment buildings looking for the man who likes to lick lemons. They don't find him, so they scatter back home for dinner.

THE PET

Basia, barefoot, in her pajamas, stood on the cold linoleum in front of the kitchen sink, an empty enamel cup in her hands. There was a flash of white fur, a long pink tail. Red eyes. She screamed and it was gone.

Impossible, Mama said. I just cleaned up the kitchen and didn't see it anywhere, she tucked the blanket around Basia and kissed her. Maybe you should read something else. The Nutcracker is too scary.

No! It's my favourite. I know it's just a book.

Ok then, but no more nonsense. She pressed her hand to Basia's forehead. You are well enough to go to school, but you can stay home since it's Friday.

Basia smiled and hugged her Mama. She would miss the school concert presented by grade three students. She had huge stage fright. Mama loved her to perform and Basia hated to disappoint her.

Mama kissed Basia, and left for work. Basia ran her hands over the pile of books on her bed, and had a sip of juice. She missed Mama already. She came every time Basia called her to bring something to drink, eat, or play with. She stood in line for hours to get expensive oranges and bananas for Basia. She cooked her favourite meals because Basia was a picky eater.

Mama spoon-fed Basia for a long time: And this for your grandma; this one for your grandpa, she said every time she forced a spoon in Basia's mouth. And this one for your mama, because you love her. Basia couldn't say no. She didn't say no to a large duck-shaped bun, whose blind stare still frightened her after she had bitten its head off. Nor to the tomato soup that later rose up like a swear word.

You ruined my dress! I spend all day cooking for you and that's how you thank me? Mama screamed, her face in red splotches. She threw the spoon. Basia wasn't allowed to leave the table until she finished eating.

She never threw up again. If vomit filled her mouth, she swallowed it.

Basia would do anything for Mama. Even washing the empty pickle jars behind the credenza that had spiders in them. If anything happened to Mama, Basia would die, like the girl from the novel *Anielka*. Basia loved books, especially those with pictures. And fairy tales. She caressed their covers, dipped into the cool pages as into jam, licking her fingers greedily as she read. Here was a drawing of Marie, in bed with a bandaged arm, a cloud above her head showing the battle between mice and dolls. Marie's parents were frowning—they didn't believe in such things.

What was that noise like tiny clocks, little feet shuffling, and a squeak, like her yellow bath duckie? Basia put her head under the blanket not daring to go the bathroom until she heard a key in the front door.

It was only lunchtime and Mama was back, glancing at her watch, fiddling with the knot of her red scarf. She touched Basia's forehead with her hand, Get up, Basia. You are going to the school concert. Important men are coming to celebrate the Leader's birthday with us. Isn't it exciting? Put on a white shirt and a navy skirt. Don't forget the red ribbon for your collar.

You told me I could stay in bed. Basia folded back her duvet and sat up reluctantly, hanging her legs over the edge of the bed. Her feet felt cold. I can't remember my poem anymore.

Basia could already see Izabela's jeering face and fat finger pointing. When they had read a dialogue in class, Izabela said, You're saying it wrong. My mother said you should do it this way. Izabela had stood up and fanned her hands as she recited. Her voice rose and fell as if climbing a row of hills. She thought she was special because her mother was a stewardess and brought her Michael Jackson tapes and jeans from the West.

I can't go, Mama. It will look strange if I go to the concert but not to class, Basia whined. Mama wouldn't listen. She checked her face in her compact and put on a fresh layer of blood-red lipstick.

Basia's stomach hurt. What if she died? Mama would be sorry. Why was the stupid concert so important anyway?

Tata would've let me stay home, Basia whispered. One day when she came back from school she had found Mama in the kitchen talking to two militiamen. Her mascara was smudged and she had red streaks on her arms. When Basia asked her what they wanted, Mama said they told her things about Tata. They had given him a choice, family or America. You are lying, Mama said to them. Wait and see, one of them answered.

Mama sighed. I have to go back to work, Basia. The show starts in two hours. I will be in the history classroom, the one with the busts, if you'd like to practice your poem, she said. She didn't kiss Basia before she left.

Basia decided to stay home. Mama was busy, and by the time she realized, it'd be too late. Why hadn't she told Basia earlier? Basia would've practiced. No one expected her to be there, she was sick.

She tried to remember the lines as she took off her pajamas. She closed her eyes and concentrated. The title and the first line came to her and then nothing. She couldn't recall a single word, as if her fever had burned it out of her mind.

Did the clock have to tick so loudly? Where were her white socks? She rummaged through her dresser drawers; balls of socks falling onto the carpet. She settled on a white pair with red stripes. Now the blouse. Mama laid out her clothes every morning, she would know where it was. She found it in Mama's closet amongst the formal wear. Why so wrinkled?

Basia didn't know how to iron, so she smoothed it out on her chest hoping Mama wouldn't notice.

She copied her poem on a piece of paper and put it in her pocket.

The school hallways were empty—classes had begun. Basia wished the stairs would never end. At each step she tried to recite a line. Scraps of phrases, such as "our esteemed Leader," "the brave liberators," and "freedom and equality for all," swam to the surface like guppies in her aquarium coming up for food, but she couldn't catch them. Their little mouths blew bubbles, but they were mute. Her hands shook and the lines blurred together. Maybe if Mama prompted her she could go on.

At last. Come in quick, Mama said, clapping her hands, white chalk dust puffing around them. There's only thirty minutes left. Recite the poem to your classmates for practice.

Basia stood up straight, exhaled, and began. She could see Izabela's smirk.

Basia's voice was caught in her throat. It scratched and squeaked. Basia could feel the tears. She tried to speak as fast as she could, hoping that the rush of words would propel her through the poem, but she got stuck after the first line. Izabela snorted. Teacher's pet—ha! she whispered.

I can't do it! Basia cried. I can't remember anything! Can I go home, Mama, please?

Go to the bathroom and calm down, Mama pointed at the door in the back of the room. Practice the poem and say it again when you're ready. And let go of your skirt, she slapped Basia's hands which held her skirt half way up her thigh.

Basia stood in front of the mirror crying. Her eyes were red, her face swollen. Everybody would know. She'd never be ready. She wouldn't go to the concert. She could hear Mama's sing-song voice praising a student. Mama didn't come to the bathroom to hug her and help her practice. She didn't love Basia anymore.

Basia read the poem twice. Maybe she'd mastered it this time. She came out of the bathroom and slouched toward Mama's class. She knocked on the door, and Mama let her in. She stood at the front but after the first line she choked and burst out crying.

See, I can't remember it! she shouted. She didn't care if her classmates saw her cry anymore, but she wouldn't be humiliated in front of the whole school. I won't go! I can't! she sobbed. She waited for Mama, who would surely be moved by her tears, to let her go home.

Look children, a big girl, and such a cry-baby! Cry-baby! Let's laugh at her. Ha, ha, ha! Mama said and the class obediently laughed along with her. She grabbed Basia's arm and pulled her out of the classroom. Control yourself at once! Wash your face. You have to go to the assembly in a few minutes and I have a lesson to finish, Mama pushed her forward. Basia stumbled towards the door, too stunned to say anything.

Basia stood on the stage in the silence of the expectant audience. Her voice shook at the title, at the first line, but the second line unfurled in her mind like a banner. She didn't even realize that she was done until she heard the clapping. Her classmates' faces were lost in the blur of spectators. She wished Tata was here.

She saw the principal pat Mama on the shoulder and introduce her to a group of balding men in green soldier uniforms. One of them put his fat arm around Mama's slim waist. Basia waved to Mama, but she had bent down to adjust her shoe strap and disappeared in a circle of men.

Let's make something special for dinner tonight to celebrate Mama said when they walked home that night.

My recitation? Basia said and skipped. She'd forgive Mama if she made her favourite cauliflower soup with sour cream.

—the Leader's birthday, Mama continued in her teacher voice. Then she looked at Basia and quickly added, and your recitation too, of course. She fixed a clip in Basia's hair.

Back at the apartment, they opened the cupboard underneath the sink to take out the dishes. Among the frying pans, pots and lids, sat a snow-white rat with red eyes staring at them.

Mama shrieked and slammed the door. They looked at each other, and then Mama opened it again. The rat was still there. Mama scared it away by banging lids on top of the counter. Then she cleaned and disinfected underneath the sink.

The next day, when Mama carried the freshly-washed white-and-red flag something white flashed across the floor. Mama screamed, dropped the flag, and skidded on the linoleum floor.

You look like an Olympic skater, I give you nine points.

Basia, go do your homework, Mama said picking up the flag.

Later that evening, Mama's head disappeared inside the

cupboard under the kitchen sink. There was a box of cement beside her, for plugging holes around water pipes.

But the next day the rat was back, inside the enamel soup pot under the sink. Mama bought a dozen "People's Brand" rat traps "guaranteed to trap vermin like the police eliminate counter-revolutionaries."

What is a counter-revolutionary? Basia asked.

Disobedient, Mama looked up fiercely from the trap in which she'd skewered a lump of bacon grease. She placed several on the kitchen counters, the floor and inside the cupboards. The next day, they found a clump of bloodied hair in one trap like an insult.

I bet Tata could catch it, Basia said.

Tata isn't here, is he?

Maybe you should tell him to come back?

It's not that easy.

Why?

He left me for the American dream. With blonde hair and long legs.

Finally Mama bought some rat poison, mixed it with kasha grain and scattered it in the apartment. A few days later Basia saw bloody footprints along the edge of the sink.

Basia's bedroom door creaked open.

Wake up darling, wake up, Mama said. You have to help me.

What? Basia rubbed her eyes in the morning light and slowly sat up.

Kill it. Use this.

She held out a broom.

Pink paws, and quivering nostrils tumbled through Basia's mind. She leaned back, her shoulder blades bumped painfully into the headboard.

What's wrong with Mama?

Basia, are you listening to me? Mama waved a hand in front of Basia's face.

No! I will not kill it for you, Basia pushed the wooden broomstick away.

Mama left the room without a word.

Basia covered her head with a pillow. She could hear the repeated bangs of the stick and the clang of pots. She imagined the rat crawling along the countertop, its fur matted with blood, slipping down onto the kitchen floor, blind, beads of blood beneath its eyes.

Everything went quiet.

Basia gave Mama enough time to throw out the body and clean up. When she came out, Mama had set the table. She stared at Basia.

Those are not the clothes I picked for you.

Basia shrugged and sat down.

They chewed in silence, without their usual argument about food. Basia nibbled at a piece of rye bread with schmaltz. She remembered the rat in biology class, in a wood chip-filled aquarium. An albino. The science teacher said they were rare, and showed Basia how to feed it out of her hand.

THE DIAMENT GIRLS

It's my turn: my sneakers press the white elastic into the dirt. I push and twirl—my braids whip my cheeks like blades as I land back on the rubber band. Chinese jump rope is my favourite. I feel my playmates' eyes: Fail, fail. It's a perfect jump, but when I line up for the next round, the girls say I failed. We ask Dorota to decide.

You made a mistake, she says without a pause, the cavity on her two upper front teeth is black and round like a wax letter seal. Her sisters, Julita, who goes to a special school and tells everybody she had a baby whom she gave up for adoption, and Iwonka, who is my age, wrap their arms around her and look at me triumphantly. For the rest of the game I stay inside the elastic band, hold it taut for the other girls, and wait for one of them to trip up.

Next we play Mother. Dorota dribbles the ball in front of us. Long shadows grow from her feet like stilts. She stops in front of me, leans forward, holding the ball. I can see her little breasts, like cupcakes, through the hanging neckline of her shirt. My heart jumps as the ball slaps the asphalt. Dorota's smile tells me that she will pick me. I smile back opening my arms. She throws the ball to the girl beside me.

Later we sit on a low cement wall at the foot of our apartment building. Dorota is singing. I wish that I could sit there all my life listening to her, imagining the song is about her and me.

Julita and Iwonka cross their arms over my back. The coolness that comes with summer dusk has tempered their characters and they don't tease me anymore. Our bare, mosquito-bitten legs press together on the narrow wall. A dirty rhyme, whispered behind a hand with chipped nail polish, tickles my ear. I finally belong.

Then Mama's voice pierces through Dorota's song. Basia, it's time for your piano lesson. The girls retract their arms from me and slip away, as if I've begun to stink. I hate Mama. I walk away from the Diament sisters. Dorota's song, suddenly mournful and longing, floats behind me as if it hasn't been interrupted by my absence.

In the evenings boys buzz around Dorota's heavy-lidded beauty like it is a sugar-coated fly strip. She lets them catch her, and then slips out of their arms like a mermaid and runs, her ill-fitting dress frothing up around her legs. Julita staggers after them, her breasts swinging underneath her T-shirt like cathedral bells, her limbs like spires. The boys don't pay any attention to her. It is Dorota whom we all want. Fat Julita, Iwonka, the Diament sister whose only distinction is her last name, and I, insignificant as the gravel under our feet, stare at Dorota with jealousy and awe from the edges of the parking lot.

A powerful trinity, the Diament sisters rule our playground: the empty car park and the rubbish bin enclosure behind our apartment building, the vacant lots overgrown with weeds, the dirt paths scribbled by our restless feet, and the labyrinthine concrete spaces of the new school permanently under construction. I tell myself I don't care about Dorota and her sisters, I don't want them to be my friends. My toys and books are enough. I remember what Mama tells me, that they swear and lie, and skip school. I'm in love with their wildness, their selfishness. Beautiful and invincible as weeds.

One day Dorota's mother comes to borrow some money. She is a petite woman with a mass of silver hair and a toothless mouth. She stands at our threshold, her arms across her chest as if she were cold. Her voice has a rasp that makes my throat feel sore, her breath smells like beer. Mrs. Diament looks at the ground when Mama calls me to the door. Basia, she says, Mrs. Diament says that she has given you the money she owes me from last month? Is that true?

Mrs. Diament looks nothing like her daughters. I often see her standing behind the beer store, laughing and drinking with the men who smoke in the shade every afternoon.

No, she hasn't, I say and watch her stoop even lower and stumble down the staircase. Mama goes back to the kitchen where she's making *barszcz*, and I sneak away to check if the money is still under my bed. Later that night I eavesdrop. Mama says to Tata, she lied to me, and she accused Basia of lying. My child! Can you imagine? I won't lend her any more money. Her husband is in prison again.

Mama is wrong. Their father is a pirate, Dorota told me. He has a beard, gold teeth, and blue tattoos of mermaids and anchors.

I'm not allowed to play with Dorota or her sisters. But I don't listen. I buy them sugar drops and chewing gum with my guilty loot, and the attention I get that day is sweeter than any candy. If one of the Diament girls wants to play badminton or soccer, I run home to get racquets or a ball. I'd rather watch them than play alone.

Each evening I hear the joyous yells of children playing with the Diament girls as I lie in bed. Tag, dodge ball, hide-and-seek. After sunset everybody will play with flashlights. In darkness, the lit faces and slim limbs will emerge, as if disembodied, from behind fences and bushes. Their parents don't make

29

them to go to sleep when it's still light outside. I amuse myself by counting the cherries and leaves scattered on the curtains.

Children become acrobats on the construction site scaffolding where I'm not allowed to play. With their dirty fingers they pinch off the caulking at the edges of windowpanes and knead it like plasticine. They scavenge for discarded drywall and draw hopscotch squares on the streets. I imagine that I'm with them, behind the garbage bin enclosure, where they hang like bats on the carpet-beating stand, spotted with pigeon droppings and rings of rust where the paint has peeled off like eczema. Apartment keys dangle on shoelaces around their necks like a secret society. I beg Mama to give me our key but she says I don't need it.

Every night Mama puts on a record of fairy tales before I go to sleep. Muddled, drowsy thoughts mesh with outside voices in dreams elaborate as my tangled morning hair. Dorota becomes an enchanted princess, then a beggar, revealed only to me, the prince, because I love her.

I'm almost asleep when I hear the Diament girls enter their apartment next door—we share my bedroom wall. I flatten my palms against the rough paint hoping that Dorota or one of her sisters does the same. I can almost feel the heat from another body coming through.

One glorious day I become one of them. I have a new doll and an older doll with a new dress. I take them outside to play on a blanket beneath our apartment windows. Dorota comes over.

I want to play with your dolls.

I nod.

Let's go somewhere where your mother can't... somewhere more fun, the playground around the corner.

I feel like I have just blown out the birthday candles, my wishes are all coming true. I gather up the blanket; Dorota carries the dolls. A few girls who have been watching us from the sidewalk want to join us, but Dorota tells them to scram. I smile at her, but she is busy examining the dolls.

We cook meals and serve them on leaves: soups made of sand and pebbles, salads of shredded grass, chamomile petals, and clover flowers. I watch Dorota on the other end of the teeter-totter, holding my doll, we are forever connected. Dorota holds my hand not minding my sweaty palms. She grins at me, and when we bend over the dolls, I feel the heat of her skin.

Let's put them to sleep on their grass beds and pick more dandelions for their breakfast, Dorota says. When we come back, the doll in the new dress is gone.

We look for it under the blanket, among the doll clothes, on the playground, in the sandbox, in the grass. We don't see it anywhere. Dorota suggests that we split up to find it faster. She is so clever.

But we don't find it. I'm unhappy because of the new dress. Dorota hugs me and rubs my back. I can feel shivers down my spine, all the way to my sandaled feet. I make myself cry so Dorota will keep holding me. I almost faint when she kisses my cheek. She promises to help me look for it tomorrow.

I sneak into my room to drop off my doll. Mama notices and I tell her what happened.

You silly girl, she says, I told you not to play with her or her sisters. I'm sure that Dorota covered your doll with grass and pretended that she didn't know where it was. Later she came back to get it.

Dorota wouldn't do such a thing. She loves me. She's helped me look for it; she hugged and kissed me. Mama tells me I'm naïve. Then she goes to talk to Mrs. Diament even though I beg her not to. She comes back with my doll and

31

triumphantly hands it to me. I turn my back to her and go to my room leaving the doll behind. Why would anyone want it?

I never play with the Diament girls again. At night I listen to the sounds in their apartment and imagine what they are doing. I think of possible excuses for Dorota. I've forgiven her already. I miss her.

When my cousin moves to our city I finally have someone to play with. Edyta is a year older than me. She wears black clothes and her blond hair is long and loose. Mama still plaits my hair in two braids with big, embarrassing bows. She buys me clothes with teddy bear and duck patterns. Edyta listens to heavy metal and goes to concerts—bands whose names I've never heard of. Her mother lets her do everything. She is beautiful and sophisticated. Like Dorota.

She tells me stories about her boyfriends, about kissing and making out. I try dressing and walking like her. She teaches me to swear and disobey Mama. I offer her my favourite toys and clothes, but she ridicules them. When I find a diamond ring in a crack in the pavement Edyta takes it from me. It's just for a day, she says when I don't want to open my palm. When I ask for it back, she tells me she has lost it. You thought it was a real diamond? It was only a cheap piece of glass, she says.

We share my bed so we can talk at night. We compare our new breasts (I still have to catch up), and legs (mine are longer). It is the one thing she envies me. Edyta steals her mother's heels to make up the difference. On the playground we pretend she is my American cousin. We talk a made-up language.

One day Edyta points to a girl in red gym shorts running in front of us.

Look at her legs. She has the most beautiful legs I've ever seen. Like a marathon runner, Edyta says.

Edyta has never praised my legs.

The girl keeps running. Her legs are long, straight and narrow in the knees and ankles. Muscular in the thighs and calves. But look at her shorts, and her T-shirt. They are fraying, Edyta sneers. These legs are all she has.

It's Dorota. Her white legs flash in the sun, then disappear into a shadow of a building.

Her name is Dorota, I say to Edyta. The fastest runner I know.

EPIDEMIC (DIRECTOR'S CUT)

1

Mama waves to Basia, shouting: Basia, honey, this is Karolina, I'm sure you will become best friends!

Clouds of dust billow behind them from the open door of the schoolhouse, which is being transformed into a dormitory for the city kids. Mountains, studded with rocks and conifers, all around. Shirtless men carrying mattresses slip in and out of the shadowed doorway. A bronze bust of Lenin looks down from the parapet of a second story window, motes of dust around his head like a halo.

This is going to be the worst summer ever. Why can't Mama let her make her own friends? Last year at the school dance Mama asked Arek, her crush, to dance with her! He refused, and Basia cried in the bathroom for the rest of the night. Basia has always wanted to have a best friend, like Anne's Diana. Now Mama has spoiled it all.

Basia would rather have stayed home with Tata, but Mama insisted—her registration is free because Mama is a camp counselor. Her brother was invited to a friend's cottage by the Baltic Sea. It's good to get out of the Warsaw smog for a couple of weeks, Mama said.

It had been a long drive to camp. The landscape slid past the bus, the windows like frames in a reel of film, the kind Basia fed into the projector with her dad every Saturday night. Tree branches clawed at the bus, scraping the paint as it navigated the narrow roads. Rising hills, like arching backs of beasts. Vehicles and people like fleas scrambling across them.

During a bathroom stop, Basia stayed on board. She noticed a pair of long, pale legs, a T-shirt logo of the band Roxette. A couple of big boys nearby pointed at the girl. One of them rocked his skinny hips. Boys are disgusting, Basia thought, and looked at her scrawny, scabby knees and furry shins, covered with bruises and mosquito bites. Later, Basia recognizes the Roxette shirt on Karolina. The mattresses and beds are from a prison, she whispers in Basia's ear and grabs her hand. Her fingers feel cool and she is wearing nail polish.

I stole it from my mama's purse, she says. Criminals slept on them, she adds. The mattresses. Guess what the stains are.

Gross, Basia says and imagines big, hairy men, their busy hands, their heavy bodies shuddering on the mattresses at night. Murderers, or worse, rapists.

I don't care if your mama is a teacher, Karolina says. This boy in my school? He smokes and swears, gets into fights. He is so cool, she sighs. His mother is the principal.

2

You can move your bed close to mine, says Karolina the first night and wiggles her toes. Her legs are sticking out through the metal bars at the foot of the bed. You don't have lice, do you?

Basia doesn't know. She did have lice, several months ago. Probably from Magda, who has thick brown hair and smells funny. She stole Basia's best friend Dominika; they sat behind her in class, whispering and giggling. One day Magda wore Basia's beret in art class, Look at me, I'm an *artiste*! She told everyone Basia couldn't have painted that picture. It was too good.

Of course I don't, Basia says, and pushes her bed. It bumps against Karolina's with a clang. Mama had soaked her hair in vinegar to kill the lice; Basia hated the acrid, sharp smell even more than its sting. Then she wrapped a towel on Basia's head and covered it with a plastic bag. Don't tell anybody you had lice, Mama said, people will think we're dirty. Basia's friends saw her looking out the window. She told them she had a migraine. She pulled the curtains shut, turned off the light. Sleeping Beauty, a 24 mm film, lit up the cracked bedroom wall skipping and rattling in the old projector. Tata promised her a new one for her next birthday.

Basia can smell Karolina's hair—chamomile. Her face looks so different sideways: slanted eyes, delicately fuzzy nostrils.

Karolina grabs Basia's hands and presses them to her chest. Do you feel them? she says. They are finally growing. Can I touch yours?

Basia's nipples hurt when Karolina presses them. She gasps.

That means they are starting, Karolina laughs.

Aunt Jolanta gave Basia a bra last Christmas. Basia only realized what it was after she'd removed the gift wrap, in front of everybody. She quickly buried it under her other presents and later stuffed it in her sock drawer. Basia hated Aunt Jolanta. She was fat, she always argued with Uncle Leon, and she had smashed Basia's favourite ornament, a red mushroom with white spots, when she sat on it.

Do you have your period yet? Karolina whispers. Her breath is warm and wet, like a puppy's, against Basia's neck.

No, says Basia. Her face burns, and she is glad it is dark.

She has been sleeping with a box of pads under her pillow for months, but nothing's happened yet. Every girl in her class already has it.

I almost got mine. It was in my ballet class. There was blood in my panties. But it only happened this one time. Maybe something broke inside me a bit, Karolina says.

Girls, it's time to sleep, Basia's mama calls from behind the partition. Karolina rolls her eyes.

Mama, can't I tell a story? Basia yells. That's what you are supposed to do at camp. Scary stories.

3

Once upon a time there lived an innkeeper who had a wife and a beautiful but disobedient daughter. She hated to sleep, so she stayed up late every night reading books, even though she said, Yes Mama, when her mother asked her to blow out the candle.

One night, when they were about to go to sleep, an old man with a cane asked for a room. They were full, but it was raining cats and dogs, so they invited him in. The daughter didn't like him, and begged her parents not to let him stay.

He is a bad man, she said.

Don't lie, they scolded her.

He made his bed out of his coat in the dining room by the fireplace.

Everybody was soon asleep. Only dogs were heard in the distant village, and a soft rumbling from people snoring in their rooms. Suddenly, the innkeeper's daughter heard a noise, like a tree branch knocking on a door. It was the old man, walking from room to room.

4

Basia and Karolina are hopping down the stairs to the cafeteria for breakfast.

You are the hottest girls in camp, a tall boy says when they pass by the older boys' dorm room. His voice skips an octave halfway through. The girls look at each other and giggle.

I want him to be my boyfriend, Karolina whispers.

Let's go, Basia says. Boys are so boring. They always want to play with cars or pretend war.

No, I want to talk to him, Karolina says and smiles at the boy. He has red hair and freckles. He grabs Karolina by her arms and drags her behind the door. The lock clicks. Karolina screams, something knocks against the door. Laughter. Then silence. Basia pulls on the door handle and pounds her fists on the door. Karolina, are you ok? Should I call someone?

Basia's friend once told her that her little sister stepped out of their apartment block elevator with her clothes ripped, blood on her thighs.

When Karolina comes out her face is red and she is tucking her shirt into her shorts. She is smirking. Please don't tell anybody, she says.

You know I won't.

You are my best friend, Karolina says and kisses Basia quickly on the lips. Basia feels a pulse, like a drum beat, in her head.

I really need to pee, Basia says and runs downstairs. Meet you in the cafeteria, she shouts over her shoulder.

It's cottage cheese salad with radishes, tomatoes, and green onions for breakfast. Basia hates it. She likes her cottage cheese with sugar and cream, rolled inside a crepe. But Karolina swears it's going to make her breasts grow bigger, so they both eat it, with second helpings.

Here is something to get rid of radish breath, Karolina says and presses a candy in a brightly-coloured wrapper into Basia's hand. My dad brought me a whole bag from East Germany, she says.

Basia slips it into the back pocket of her shorts. A keepsake.

5

The innkeeper's daughter quietly slipped out of bed and followed the old man. She had learned to be very quiet so her mama would think she was asleep.

The old man went to the first room in the inn. Wake up, he whispered, and when the doctor who was sleeping there sat up in bed, the old man cut his throat with a sling blade so fast that he didn't make a sound. The innkeeper's daughter was too terrified to scream. She followed him to the next room. He whispered, Wake up, but the soldier who was sleeping there didn't wake up. The old man shook his bed. The soldier woke up. The old man slit his throat.

The girl quickly ran to her bedroom and hid under the covers. She could hear the old man's cane thump, thump on the floor as he entered every room in the house. Then she heard it outside her door.

6

Basia grimaces as the nurse's fingers part and tug her hair. The nurse is taking too long. She has now asked the other nurse to look. Basia can feel their breaths, smelling of schmaltz, on the back of her neck. A nit, one of them says. Basia blinks her eyes to stop the tears. She smiles at Karolina who is watching on the other side of the glass window as if they are in a silent film.

The day before, in front of the nurse's office, Basia saw a group of kids with their heads wrapped in towels. The sharp scent of vinegar drifted down the hallway. They must be those kids from the orphanage, Karolina whispered. They are so dirty.

What, you aren't crying because of lice, are you? Basia's mama asked the turbaned kids, on the way out to the park with her group.

No, *Pani* Kowalczyk, we are laughing, we are telling jokes.

Back in her room, Basia grabs her mama's hands. Send me home, Mama. Tata can pick me up. I would rather stay home all summer. Please, Mama, Basia presses her wet face into Mama's grey sweatshirt. Basia's favourite. It came from America in one of the church packages.

I can't honey, Mama pushes her gently away and looks into her face. Your father—

Then cut off my hair! Basia sobs.

Don't be ridiculous, it's just a little bit of vinegar, that's all.

You don't understand anything! Her only hope is that Mama will take her group, including Karolina, out when Basia has a stinking rag on her head. Mama always takes them somewhere: the drinking spa, where water in ceramic bird-shaped bottles tastes like rotten eggs, and toothless old men stare at Basia; to a pond in a valley, the water green and smooth like a plate. Basia tried to take a photo of it with the camera her father lent her, but it wouldn't work. She carried it into a shade of a large pine, and opened it to see what was wrong. Her film was empty, as if she'd taken photos of shadows. She was tired of all these trips. Why doesn't her mama just let them play in the yard and she can sit with the teachers in the lounge or at the tables under the linden tree?

7

Basia sits alone in the nurse's office with her wet and stinky hair.

I thought you might want Karolina for company, her mama says, beaming.

Karolina gives Basia an accusing glare.

I'm fine, Basia says. She wishes she could disappear beneath the cracked linoleum tiles. See you later? She mumbles to Karolina, but her friend has already turned away, her arm around another girl's waist.

8

That night Karolina drags her bed away from Basia's. Its metal legs screech on the floor tiles.

Basia, we all want to hear the end of your story, Mama calls out.

Kiss-ass! Karolina hisses.

9

The innkeeper's daughter lay as still as she could while the knocking of the cane came nearer and nearer. The old man bent over listening to her breathing. Wake up, he said, but the girl didn't move. He pulled off her blankets and opened the window. The cold made her body shiver. But she didn't stir. He pounded the floor with his cane. She was still. Then he raised the cane with both hands and crashed it down on her. She wanted to scream, the pain in her back was terrible, but she pretended to be asleep.

What a bunch of baloney! Karolina says loudly. She would have moved by now! Nobody sleeps that hard. The old man would have known she is pretending! The little liar that she is.

He should slit her throat.

It's fiction, Basia says.

What's fiction? Karolina asks.

It's like...lies, but they aren't bad, Basia says.

Yeah, you would know, Karolina says. I'm going to sleep, she turns her back toward Basia.

10

Basia tells Mama that Karolina hates her, that she wants to go home to Tata. It's your fault! Don't touch me, she shouts when her mama hugs her. Don't talk to me again, I am just another camper, do you understand?

Basia plays hopscotch alone. She eats mulberries from the trees growing in the shade behind the school. She lies on her bed reading stories. Karolina's bed is empty—she is out playing with Ela, who has long blond hair and breasts, and Ania, skinny as a stick, with transparent skin and dark circles under her eyes. A bunch of boys follow them around, flip their skirts up, wrestle them to the ground. They scream and laugh. They smoke cigarettes, which they buy from a local boy behind the stinking outhouse. Basia kicks Karolina's bedside table. A bag of candies falls on the floor.

In the yard, Basia sits weaving dandelions and chamomiles into a wreath. She wishes she could give one to Karolina. A younger boy from Basia's group crouches beside her.

What do you want? she asks.

Do you know my brother Edek? He has long black hair and a scar over his left eye? He fell off the fence when trying to run away?

Oh, yeah, I saw him around, she shrugs her shoulders. What about him?

43

He is in love with you, the boy says.
Basia lifts up a chamomile and sniffs it. She misses Karolina.
Do you love him?
What?
Do you love him? He loves you.
You guys are orphans? she asks.
He nods and sniffles.
Ok, you can tell him I love him, she says, blushing. It's a lie. A good lie.

11

Playing Robin Hood with Edek is fun for a while. Basia makes bows with branches and pieces of string she found in the garbage. They run in the mulberry orchard behind the school, shooting arrows and eating berries that look like white worms. They taste strong, like medicine. After several days she is bored. Edek runs off with other boys.

Basia is hungry. She pulls out a candy from her pocket. It's melted onto the wrapper. She looks up and sees Karolina, staring. The candy in her throat is like a plum stone. Karolina turns away kicking up a spray of gravel that lashes Basia in the shins.

12

You thief, Karolina pushes Basia against the wall behind her bed. You stole my candy, I saw you! Her sun-browned fingers leave red marks on Basia's arms. Ela and Ania stand behind her, hands on hips.

I didn't, says Basia.

Liar! Karolina screeches. She pulls out the colorful plastic bag from her bedside table. Look, she says waving it in front of

Ela and Ania, only four left!

I only had the one you gave me, Basia says. She can still taste it. Sickly sweet.

I never gave you any, Karolina says. You are a dirty liar. So is your Mama.

My mama is not dirty!

She always wears the same clothes!

She—she has two sweatshirts that are the same, Basia says.

That's the stupidest thing I ever heard, laughs Karolina.

I saw you looking through Karolina's stuff, says Ela. Yesterday after lunch.

Look at her face, says Ania. It's so red.

Let's go girls, Karolina says. Teacher's pet needs to cry to her mommy.

13

The old man was very angry. The innkeeper's daughter slept so deeply that nothing seemed to wake her. As long as she was asleep, he couldn't kill her. She heard him stomp back and forth beside her bed. Then he chuckled. He lit her candle. He put the flame to the soles of her feet, until her skin burned and blistered and the smell of burnt flesh filled the room. But she bit her pillow and pretended to sleep. The old man cried with frustration and rage. He walked out of the inn, and was never seen again. The innkeeper's daughter got up and ran to wake up her parents. She told them what happened and showed them her feet. She was saved by her lies.

14

Basia, come play Robin Hood? Edek asks the next day. He is standing in the doorway to Basia's room. She is memorizing a poem to recite at the camp's closing ceremony, and the introductions she will do as the MC. The town mayor is coming.

Basia doesn't even look up.

Basia? Please?

Edek can be so annoying.

So that's how it is, he says. You don't want to go together anymore?

No I don't, says Basia.

He stands there mute, except for his phlegmy breathing. What is he waiting for?

Fine, he says.

Basia is relieved.

15

On the evening of the concert, Basia looks for Mama to ask her where her navy blue dress is. But Mama has disappeared again. So Basia wears her favorite terry-cloth rainbow-coloured t-shirt and pink shorts. Red sneakers that Tata bought her last time he went abroad. She can follow others to the town hall. Otherwise she won't know where to go. Perhaps Mama is already there.

The drama teacher slides her gaze over Basia, grimaces and quickly whispers with the organist.

Change of plans dear, she says to Basia, and leads her to stand at the back, behind all the other kids who are going to recite poems. We have a new, important task for you, she says, you are going to help *Pan* Witak screen the film he made of camp. Ok? And when your turn comes, you can recite from where you are. No need to go to the front, she says.

Basia tries not to cry as she presses the button to start the film. If she were the director, Karolina would be the star, and Basia the best supporting actress. Two best friends in a boarding school. Orphans. She would nurse Karolina, sick with the plague. Basia would save her life but succumb to the epidemic herself.

The film lights up the screen. Her mama appears in one scene, tying her shoe. The tops of her breasts flash white as she bends down. *Pan* Witak swallows loudly behind Basia. It's like she's been cut from all the scenes.

She must have done something wrong, but what?

The new MC is a blond little girl in a beautiful, white lace dress.

When Basia's turn comes, she stutters, forgets her lines. She can't find Mama in the audience.

16

Where were you? Basia asks when she gets back to the dorm.

Is that what you wore to the concert? Mama asks.

You told me I look beautiful in it, Basia runs her hands over her belly. The fabric feels so soft.

Why didn't you wear your dress?

I looked for you, Basia says. You told me you would be there.

I had to take Ela to the infirmary. She has a stomach ache. I hope it's not contagious.

Why does it matter so much what I wore, Basia thinks. The girl at the concert had a white dress on. Mama is wearing her grey sweatshirt.

You lied, Basia says.

Don't be such a baby. I would have come if I could, Mama says. It's late, go to bed.

I hate your sweatshirt, Basia says.

DELETED SCENES

1

Basia's Mama is folding Basia's navy dress into an open suitcase in her bedroom at home. Basia is outside, jumping rope, chanting rhymes.

Do you think it's a good idea, Magda? Her husband emerges from the bathroom. His face half covered with shaving cream. A razor in one hand. He puts his arm around her.

Yes. Otherwise she will cry and not eat for days, like last time. She will enjoy camp, I will tell her when we get back.

Are you sure? She is older now.

Just bring her a Barbie and a pair of jeans. Or, maybe you will send for us this time.

She sighs and embraces him.

2

Karolina and the red-haired boy stare at the locked door. He looks back over his shoulder and grins at his roommates, who make kissing noises.

Is this your new girlfriend? One of them asks and sniggers.

The boy glances at Karolina and looks away. She stares at the ceiling, then at her shoes.

Are you alright? The door handle jerks. Karolina can hear Basia on the other side pounding on the door.

Karolina rolls her eyes.

The boy scratches his scalp vigorously.

Karolina quickly pulls her shirt out of her shorts and opens a few buttons. She shakes her head to loosen her hair.

See ya, she whispers and unlocks the door.

3

It's late at night. The girls are sleeping in their beds. Basia's mama leaves the room and goes out into the hallway. The teacher's lounge door is slightly ajar—a triangular blade of light slices the floor. *Pan* Witak steps outside, lights a cigarette. Dust motes float in the air around him. He is shirtless and has thick black chest hair.

Magda, I was looking for you. Would you like to join us? he asks. Behind him, Magda sees *Pani* Mazurek, the nurse, dancing on top of the coffee table. She is wearing only her panties, a bottle of Stolichnaya in her hand.

You have beautiful breasts, *Pan* Witak says.

I'm really tired, Magda says, and makes her escape.

4

Ania is crouched drawing hopscotch with a stick in the dirt. A boy walks over and touches her back.

Do you know my brother Edek?

Yeah, what about him, she says.

We are orphans.

So? She is busy drawing a 3. The stick snaps on a rock.

He is in love with you.

So? Ania stands up and scans the ground.

Do you love him?

Nope, she says. She walks over to a birch tree and breaks off a branch.

Hey, he shouts.

Yeah?

Do you know where Ela is?

5

Basia is kneeling in front of Karolina's bed. She is stuffing the candy that spilled back into the bag. Then she puts it on the bedside table. She takes her book off Karolina's bed.

Ela is watching from the doorway.

Hi, she says when Basia passes by her.

When Basia is gone, Ela closes the room door and picks up the bag of candy.

6

Basia's father is at the Warsaw Airport. He is being interviewed before being allowed to board the plane for New York City.

Sign here, says the public security official. You will return to the Polish People's Republic, when your visa expires.

Basia's father takes the pen, signs it. Then he walks towards the gate and doesn't look back.

PORTRAIT

Basia has a photograph of herself on her grandfather's lap, taken by her mother. She's wearing a white dress that barely reaches her knees. In her hair are two large white bows. Her perfectly smooth bangs, like a curtain, cast off the light of the flash. She is smiling. If you look closely you will see her grandfather's hands casually hidden underneath her dress.

Basia doesn't trust her memories. They are like the sandwiches she thinks she remembers: neatly trimmed, stripped of hard crusts, fragmented. Made palatable by her mother's quick fingers.

What are you doing, mom? seven-year-old Basia asked.

I'm making sandwiches for your Grandpa. He should be here any minute. Take your elbows off the table, please.

But why are they so funny? Why did you cut off the crusts? Basia picked the crusts off the cutting board and swirled them in the air. A piece broke off and fell on the floor.

Careful, Basia. Watch the knife—your fingers. It's because Grandpa has lost a lot of teeth. They're easier to chew. Grandpa had surgery and now his stomach's very small, he can eat only a little at a time.

They look so pretty, mom. Why d'you never make them for me? Can I have some? Basia watched her mother's agile fingers arrange the sandwiches like a puzzle on a plate.

Basia, really. I've no time to do that now. These are for Grandpa. Besides, sandwiches with crusts are good for your teeth. Grandpa's still a little sick, you know that. That is why we all must be very nice to him, quiet and attentive to what he says. Can you do that for me?

All right. But can you make me a sandwich like that, please? I really want one! Surely, the triangular sandwiches tasted better. Why couldn't she have one? Her mother had been talking about Grandpa all day. She made Basia move into her little brother's room so Grandpa could have her bed. She hadn't asked Basia if she was hungry.

Basia's grandfather was an amateur painter. He said he would love to paint Basia when she is older. When would she be sufficiently older? She looked at portraits of women in art books and imagined herself in their place.

After her grandfather died, Basia's parents found several unfinished, crude nudes—bad imitations of Balthus—in his apartment, among landscapes and still lifes. The paintings were distributed among the family; all except the nudes, they were thrown out.

The doorbell rang. Basia forgot her worries and ran to the door.

Hello my sweet girlie. Grandpa always said that. She embraced him, but when she tried to pull away he held her closer.

Give your Grandpa a kiss.

Basia recoiled. He tasted like cigarettes, and had a thick, prune-coloured growth on his lower lip. Basia became sick to her stomach when she felt the bulge, like a swollen finger. No one else kissed her on her lips, not even her parents. Maybe it was something that grandfathers did, but she had no memory of her other grandfather—he'd died before she was born.

Grandpa is here! She shouted to her mother, hoping that he'd release her when he heard her mother coming from the kitchen.

Grandfather always brought her the same present, an assortment of red plastic accessories: a necklace, bracelet, and a ring, but she was pleased to get them, because she lost them after each visit. Her grandfather helped her fasten the necklace, told her she looked like a lady. Basia admired herself in the hallway mirror and yes, she did look taller than the last time she checked. Maybe soon she could wear lipstick? She'd ask mom.

Mom, I've a stomach ache, Basia complained again, playing with her food at dinner, moping, and wandering from room to room uninterested in her toys or books.

When did you last go for number two? her mother asked, as she put her palm to Basia's forehead in a maternal reflex, in the same way she placed a hand under Basia's sweater to check if she was sweaty, or spat on a tea towel to wipe her face. Her pantomime of love.

I don't remember.
Did you go today?
No.
Yesterday?
No.
Well, I think that we should see a doctor, just to be safe.

They waited in a room that smelled acrid and soapy, with tiny hexagonal mosaic tiles on the floor. Basia was nervous when the doctor called them in. He was bone-thin, his white coat like a deflated balloon.

Hello! Is this beautiful girl my patient? he asked smiling at Basia.

This is Basia, her mother answered, nudging her forward.

Please, sit down...Not here, there, he said to her mother, who, in her confusion, had dropped her gloves. She sat meekly beneath a display of plastic internal organs like hunting trophies. The doctor told Basia to sit on top of a blue examining table.

How old are you Basia? he asked, twirling a pen in his fingers.

She is seven, and very bright. She's skipped a grade. She is very talented: she writes poetry and is an artist. Recite one of your poems for the doctor, honey. Basia put on her practiced smile, looked at her mother for a nod of approval and began her usual performance. She chose a poem that her relatives had liked at her grandfather's birthday party last year. When she'd finished, she glanced at her mother again to check if she wanted her to do anything more.

In the evening, grandfather came to Basia's bedroom to say goodnight. Basia had been reading Russian folktales. The head of her bed was near the door, so she had no time to move when her grandfather hunched over and kissed her lips. His hands slipped underneath her comforter and searched among the sheets for the bottom of her T-shirt.

Tickle, tickle, tickle, he whispered breathily. His gasps were pungent, as if something had died inside him. Basia tried to grab his hands. But his tickling became more vicious and violent, like snake bites. His fingers jabbed her in the ribs, explored her belly and chest. She squirmed and pretended to laugh, so that he wouldn't know she didn't like it. Her mother had told her to be polite and obedient to Grandpa.

Her mother wanted her to impress the doctor, so Basia was on her best behaviour. She smiled, spoke clearly when answering his questions, breathed slow or fast, depending on what he wanted. She didn't flinch when he pressed the cold plate of the stethoscope to her chest.

She stuck out her tongue as far as she could without appearing impolite. She turned her head so it would be easier to look in her ears. Once in awhile she glanced at her mother to see if she looked pleased. She did. Basia smiled at her and jumped off the table. Her stomach ache had gone away.

When Basia's parents went shopping downtown they asked her grandfather to babysit. Basia and her brother ran around the apartment playing war, shooting plastic guns, throwing imaginary grenades. The grandfather got off the armchair and grabbed her arm. His faced flushed.

Can't you be quiet, child? he shouted and dragged her to her bedroom.

Lie down, he pointed at the bed. No, not like that, face down.

Basia knew what was coming. Her father spanked her occasionally, but she accepted it as his right because he was her father, and fathers, as she'd discussed with her friends, did that when they came from work late and tired. But her grandfather had no such right. He was someone who visited her occasionally and didn't really know her. It was not his house. Yet, she did as he asked, her mother had told her to listen to him.

She closed her eyes and waited for the familiar metallic clinking of the belt buckle, and the swish of the belt released from its loops, like that of a snake chafing its skin against grass. But none came. Instead, her grandfather told her to pull down her pants. Basia hesitated. Her father never hit her on her bare bottom.

Take off your pants, grandfather insisted. Basia's anger turned into humiliation. But she raised her hips, and without looking at him, without lifting her face off the bed, pulled her pants and underwear down in a single tug. Then she waited for the sting of the belt. In the confusing silence that followed she

55

heard her grandfather's deep breathing. She could feel the heat of his breath on her skin, as if he'd hunched really close over her, waiting. Basia wouldn't ask for mercy. She would never do that. And then the slaps came: slow and deliberate, leaving a burning sensation on her buttocks, like a sticky bandage roughly pulled. A few more times, and it was over. It wasn't that painful, because he'd used his hand, but she'd almost cried. She wished she could hide somewhere where no one could see her, especially her grandfather. She was afraid that from now on every time they looked at each other, they would relive this moment.

She would not cry in front of him. Never. She waited until he left, and then got up and pulled her pants back on. She found her little brother underneath the table in the living room. She told him to come out and play quietly with his toy soldiers while she got her sketchbook and drew. She drew Koschei, the Skeleton-Man from Russian tales, whose soul was separate from his body. It was hidden inside a needle, inside an egg, inside a duck, which was inside a hare locked in a trunk, and buried underneath an oak tree. She also drew herself and her brother running away.

After a while her grandfather came over. Basia acted as if she didn't see him. How dare he shout at her and spank her as if she were a little girl. He could've told her to be quiet, and she'd have understood.

What are you doing, Basia? he asked, trying to be nice. Basia bent lower over her paper, and pretended she hadn't heard him. He sat down beside her, and looked at her picture.

Basia, your boys and girls look the same. You got it all wrong.

Basia paused, her crayon suspended over the paper. She moved her hand over the drawing and spread her fingers to cover it.

You should observe closely Basia. You would see that boys and girls are different between the legs, and you should draw them differently. Boys have a bulge in their pants. Have you never noticed?

Grandfather was so silly. Of course she knew that boys were different from girls. She helped her mother bathe her little brother many times. But in her picture boys and girls both wore jeans. The girls had long hair, braids, pig tails, or pony tails with bows, while the boys had short hair or baseball caps. Grandpa was confused because he was old.

Let me show you, he said and grabbed her hand. Basia dropped her crayon, and ran to her bedroom. She slammed the door behind her to let him know he was not to follow her.

When Basia's parents came back, she was too ashamed to tell them her grandfather had spanked her. She thought they would be angry. Grandfather didn't say anything either. She was grateful for his silence and forgave him.

On Basia's mother's birthday, her mother took her to him to have her portrait painted. Basia didn't visit him often. His apartment was different. It smelled of cologne, cigarettes, and something else, like an unfinished basement. The furniture was an intense indigo colour, made of plastic, and shiny like a mirror. A matching blue coffee table squatted in front of the couch, and blue shelving units ran along the walls. On the shelves sat stuffed birds and rabbits with aggressive glass eyes, and a few dolls. A fabric Barbie-like doll reclined in a strange pose: her arms stretched behind her back, one of her legs was bent at the knee; the other, extended. Her head was thrown back, so that her red yarn hair reached down to her hands. Another doll, imprisoned in a see-through plastic tube, was a peasant girl in traditional costume like the one Basia wore at Easter. On the top shelf stood a matryoshka doll, which Basia had an irrepressible urge to open. She wanted to play with the dolls, but her grandfather said no. Why wouldn't he let her? She was his only granddaughter, and boys didn't play with dolls, especially grown-up boys.

Basia's mother told her to be an obedient portrait sitter. She would be back in a couple of hours, she said, kissed her and left. Basia looked around for a place to sit, while her grandfather went to his bedroom to get his big trunk of art supplies. The living room was messy. Bathrobes, towels, odd socks and newspapers draped over the chairs and the couch; ashtrays, cigarette packets, and empty bottles were scattered on the coffee table, the credenza, the corner desk, the floor. Basia wanted to peel back the layers to see what was underneath. But she was afraid her grandfather wouldn't like it if she touched his things, so she added her own coat to the top of a ghost-like pile, and found a small bare patch on the couch to sit.

It would be so much easier if Basia could remember exactly what happened next. Perhaps her grandfather brought out an easel. She hadn't seen one before, so perhaps she watched with fascination while he adjusted the position of the canvas sliding the wooden plank up and down, as he opened the box of paints tubes, brushes of all sizes, and a needle as large as a pen, with which he pricked each tube until it oozed thick globs of paint. Perhaps he told Basia to sit still on a stool, while he sketched her face with charcoal, telling her not to fidget or squint, to tilt her head this way or that when she accidentally changed her pose.

Was she bored when her grandfather suggested a break? In the kitchen, while he made her an egg sandwich, he might have said:

I have an idea. Let's paint another picture of you, not just a portrait, but something much more special, something that will be a surprise. We'll keep it secret until it's finished. It will be a figure study of you. You'll like it, I promise.

All right, Basia agreed, although she had no idea what he meant. And afterwards, can I play with your dolls?

If you are good and do what I tell you. Basia smiled, the dolls would be hers, at last.

The doctor said something quickly to her mother. It sounded like nail exam. Basia looked at her mother.

Turn this way darling, her mother said, grabbed Basia's arms, and bent her over the examining table, facing the wall. Basia heard voices behind her, voices which weren't her mother's or the doctor's. A group of medical students, laughing and talking, must have entered the office. Basia wanted to turn around and see them, but her mother held her firmly in place.

Everything became a rolling boil of sound and sensation, as if Basia had fallen underwater and didn't have enough time to realize what was happening to her. Someone pulled down her panties and roughly spread her buttocks. Something long and fat pushed inside her. She clenched around the strange pressure, the feeling of invasion beyond her comprehension. She couldn't move. All she could see were the cracks and bumps in the paint on the wall in front of her, and then everything went out of focus and was lost in blankness, like the white kitchen floor tiles beneath a puddle of spilled milk, that time Basia had dropped her glass on the floor, and her mother had yelled at her.

Basia had broken into small pieces and couldn't find them. Her hands, wrists, her feet and buttocks scattered too far apart. Her face felt hot. She wanted to call her mother for help, but her mother was holding her down. She could have warned Basia, explained it to her.

Basia knew she wasn't supposed to pull up her skirt to fix her stockings in public, so someone's hand beneath her skirt didn't seem right. She felt this way the time she'd peed outside, by a construction fence around the new school. She hadn't had enough time to get home. For long time afterwards she had nightmares of boys watching her pee, laughing at her, with her skirt hitched up around her waist and her underpants at her knees.

Slowly, Basia could feel again. First, her mother's fingers still tight around her wrists. And the pushing, like a thick worm, still inside her. The cold air on her naked bottom. Goosebumps.

And then Basia fell back into numbness as if her whole body was switching on and off. She found herself dressed and facing the doctor and her mother. She wanted to cry, but everyone acted as if nothing was wrong, nothing had changed. Basia didn't cry even though she felt shaky, like when she had a fever and wanted to sleep all day.

Did he have to convince Basia to do what he wanted? Perhaps he coaxed her slowly out of her clothes, till she was wearing only her underwear, or his own bathrobe, too big for her and falling open in the front, and then nothing at all? Did she mind? Did she feel shame? Maybe she pretended not to and she smiled, like in the photograph, wearing only two white bows in her hair. She thinks he might have shown her an art album, filled with half-dressed nymphets spread languidly over couches, their long, pale limbs dipping into the heavy, curtained air like sleek oars; girls lying on the floor, naked, looking curiously into hand-held mirrors; girls playing with cats on luxurious carpets, their skirts in disarray, crumpled flowers with white pistil legs... Basia thought the pictures were strange, she was a girl just like them and at the same time not like them at all. They looked half-asleep, feverish, sick.

Did he watch Basia undress, or did he help her take off her clothes, and his fingers casually brushing against her tiny nipples, and her thin, goose-skinned thighs? Did he pose her, reclining on the couch, in these mawkish gestures?

What she does remember—Grandpa offering her candies from a fish-shaped bowl teetering on its long glass stem. They were oval with a bumpy surface. They stuck together. She had to break one off. At first it tasted like dust, and then sickeningly sweet. She does not remember if she got to play with the dolls.

BOZIA

Stanisława smiles into the flash. She loves having her photo taken—her Mama has so few pictures of Stasia in the house. They are mostly her class photographs, several from the grade she had to repeat, in which she looks progressively older, and the one from her First Communion in Mama's bedroom, between the wooden crucifix and the white rectangle on the wall where Stalin's picture used to hang.

Stasia's face hurts and her lips feel like someone has yanked them, so she isn't sure if the picture will turn out.

Hey, look. She's smiling, the taller one laughs. He has a long face and the mouth of a grasshopper. He said his name is officer Sadow-something, when he picked her up at her house at sunrise.

Turn to your right, and hold the card straight, he tells her.

Look at these teeth. I'm amazed they don't fall out when she talks. She's the only one we have? says the other one, as he rubs his jaw with his hand, dimpled like a baby's, but with dirty fingernails.

Unfortunately. The others disappeared like blood in the sand.

Stasia likes looking at people's hands. On a rare bus trip to the city to visit Mama's cousin Magda and her children, she saw a man with six fingers on each hand, like her cat. It would be nice to have more fingers. She could wear more rings. Mama always buys her a new ring at the fall kermis. They sell gold ones with sparkly coloured stones, and small silver ones with glass over pictures of animals, flowers, or hearts. These are her favourites, because the band is open to adjust the size.

Now turn to the left, and we're done, says the fat one. His name is something like Kowalski or Kowalczyk. Stasia has problems remembering long words or names.

We'll probably have to take these again, when the swelling goes down, Grasshopper says.

Stasia yawns. It's been a long night, and a confusing day. She can barely see the trees out the window—the solitary streetlamp in front of the police station is broken. She hasn't eaten anything since last evening, except a rye bread sandwich with schmaltz and homemade pickle, which Fatty threw on the table. You have a very loving mother, he said. She'd do anything to help you, and I mean anything a man would want. At least *Pani* Zuza, a woman in a blue cardigan at one of the desks, gave her barley coffee. It's in a glass nestled in the same aluminum basket with a small handle like Stasia has at home. It pinches her fingers when she lifts it. Why hasn't her Mama come to get her? Where is Marek? He promised they'd never be apart.

Stasia has left her coffee in the bright office at the back of the station, so she's glad when she feels Grasshopper's hand between her shoulder blades steering her back there. The padded chairs inside are more comfortable than the metal bench in the windowless room where she's been trying to sleep. She prayed her mama or Marek would come to get her. Mama always says you'll sleep as well as you've made your bed, but they didn't give her any sheets.

Look here Stasia, we need to go over your statement from this morning. We still have a lot of questions. *Pani* Zuza is going to write down what you say this time. Officer Grasshopper nods towards *Pani* Zuza, who carries a machine and a stack of paper into the room. The machine is grey, with several rows of white buttons on top, which Stasia's fingers itch to press. She squirms in her seat and bites her fingernails.

Grasshopper reads a sheet of paper in front of her: Marek said he'd give me a diamond ring. It was dark. I couldn't see her. I hit. I hit hard. Everywhere. There were screams. My stick broke. But we were wrong. *Pani* Góraj is not a bad person. Now I know. Bozia punished us. We ran. I was left behind. Where is Marek? He said he loved me. We are going to be married. Łukasz found me.

I'm sorry, he shakes his head. We have to start from the beginning, he says. How old are you, Stanisława?

18.

Are you still at school? Working?

I finished grade eight. Mama says thank God for that, it took long enough. I'm better with my hands. I can weed a garden real well, I can bake a poppy seed cake, and I make the best sandcastles.

Fatty snorts. Grasshopper ignores him and turns to Stasia: That's very good, Stasia. Just remember, what we ask you is very important, so you have to tell the truth. Do you understand?

Yes, Mama says that lies have short legs.

You have a smart Mama. Now, let's get some facts straight. You were born in 1970, in the village of Ciemno, near Radom. You live with your mother and your brother Łukasz. Do you get along with him? asks officer Grasshopper.

He doesn't like me, Stasia looks down at the table and scratches at a dent. I want to be a good girl for him and Mama.

65

I didn't know it was wrong. Łukasz gets so mad. He hits me. But the foam tasted so good. I was hungry so I went to the pub after school. And the nice man at the counter gave me sips while I sat on his lap. Łukasz found me and screamed at the man, and then he slapped me. Stasia starts to cry and puts her hand to her cheek.

We won't talk about it anymore. *Pani* Zuza, do you have a handkerchief? *Pani* Zuza passes Stasia a square of white linen with an embroidered border.

What about your father? asks Fatty.

I don't have a daddy, Mama says.

He's the guy we arrested a couple of years ago for statutory rape. Same name, same underbite. Remember? Grasshopper whispers to Fatty.

What is rape? Are you talking about Marek? Stasia asks.

There was another report—attempted rape—he chased a woman across her potato field, but she managed to escape and locked herself in a tool shed. She filed a complaint about her damaged crop, continues Grasshopper.

Stasia sighs. They don't answer her questions and ask so many. It isn't fair. She licks her black fingers. They have no flavor. The officers pressed them on a damp pad and then some paper after they took her pictures.

Oh yeah, Cezar the Chaser, they called him in the village, chuckles Fatty. *Pani* Zuza stops pressing the buttons on the machine that cluck like hens, and looks at the officers the same way Mama looks at the village men who drink vodka in front of the church after Sunday mass.

Officer Grasshopper clears his throat. Last night, did you, Marek and Łukasz go to *Pani* Góraj's house? he asks.

Yes. I, Marek, and a few of his friends: Jan, Jacek, and Olek. But Łukasz wasn't with us.

Can you tell us who is Marek again? Grasshopper leans across the table so close that Stasia can smell his breath—hunter's stew sauerkraut. Her mother makes the best *bigos*, with dried prunes. I want my mother, why isn't she here? Stasia cries. Where's Marek, why won't you let him see me? She turns towards Grasshopper.

That's what we want to know, says Fatty and glances at Grasshopper.

Marek is my boyfriend. He loves me very much. He bought me a chocolate bar. Snickers. They are expensive. And a card that says I love you in large pink letters and plays a song when you open it. I keep it in my room in my super special secret box. I can show it to you if you come over. Marek said that after I kill the witch he's gonna buy me a pair of jeans and marry me. I am his girl, his best girl. I am the only girl in the gang you know. The only one who passed the test.

What test? Grasshopper and Fatty jump in their seats.

The test you need to pass to join Marek's gang. After school we climbed inside the classroom through an open window. They told me to lie down on a desk with my knees up. Two girls held my arms, Marek's friends held my feet.

Then Marek took out a chalk from a drawer in the teacher's desk. He pulled up my dress.

Her legs had goose-bumps from the open window. Marek's hands felt like hot embers that burn her every time she stokes the fire in the oven.

And he—Stasia giggles. Saliva runs out the corners of her mouth, down the sides of her protruding jaw—he put the chalk between my legs.

At first it hurt a bit. But Stasia was brave and didn't cry. Then she felt ticklish, hot and wet, when Marek wiggled the chalk around. She thought she'd peed herself.

Then the other boys did it as well. But before they were finished Łukasz jumped into the room. His face was red like a copper pot. He hit Marek in the face so hard he was bleeding and his nose swelled up like a sausage. The girls let go of my hands and ran to the window. The boys followed. Marek too, even though I asked him to stay. Quit staring like a calf at a painted gate, Łukasz said and slapped my face. He called me a whore. I think it means something bad. Then we went home.

Stasia had cried all the way home. She was afraid, because of Łukasz, she wouldn't be able to join the gang. He might tell Mama.

So how did you end up in the gang? Fatty pulls a *Popularne* cigarette out of a paper box in his front jacket pocket. When he lights up his hands tremble. *Pani* Zuza shakes her head and looks down at the paper stuck in the machine.

The next day Marek told me I'd passed the test. He told me to meet him in the old park behind the school. When I got there he was alone. He shoved me on the ground. He pulled down my panties and made pee inside me.

Stasia grabbed at the grass blades under her palms. They felt like tiny knives. The air smelled like earth and milk. The tips of pines swayed in the sky above Marek's body.

He what? Fatty smirks at Grasshopper. *Pani* Zuza's hands hover over the white buttons of the machine. Her lips are tight.

He peed inside me. Stasia is surprised they don't understand. Marek said that everyone does it. Don't you, with your wife? she asks Grasshopper. Fatty chuckles.

What happened at *Pani* Góraj's place? Why her?

Pani Góraj is a witch. She cast an evil eye on *Pan* Kaczynski's cow. It lay in the barn all day, didn't eat and swelled-up like a bladder. *Pan* Kaczynski had to pay her to break the curse. She sprinkled holy water around the cow and whispered spells.

Then she tied dried horseradish root around the animal's neck and said it would be well in two days. After two days the cow got up and started chewing grass as if nothing happened. It even got milked the same day, but *Pan* Kaczynski threw out the milk just in case it was poisonous.

And when pregnant *Pani* Małaczek ignored *Pani* Góraj's greeting, the witch put a curse on her. The baby came early and it was a changeling with slanted eyes. He's now four and doesn't talk; he only makes strange animal sounds.

Pani Góraj has beehives and has never been stung. She sings spells to them to keep them tame when she collects the honey. And when old Maciej stole and drank all her mead, he was poisoned and slept for a week. It's a miracle that he even woke up, Stasia shivers. The bees always scared her most.

People say that *Pani* Góraj killed her son, she continues. She pushed him into her well when he wanted to leave for America. Everybody knows he didn't get to America because he'd have sent her money and she'd be rich. But she's the only one in the village who lives under a thatched roof and wears winter boots all year round. Marek says that she doesn't need money from America. She can make gold, and besides, people pay her to banish evil, remove spells or cast them on their neighbours, or heal them. Marek says she doesn't deserve her wealth. He says that we should take it and give it back to the people, that we will be heroes, like Janosik. Do you know Janosik, officer? He lives in the Tatry Mountains and he steals from the rich and gives to the poor.

Yes, yes, I know of him. Tell us what happened next, officer Grasshopper shakes his hand at her, as if trying to wave off bees.

Marek and the other boys—

Their names?

Oh, I don't remember. I think Jacek, Olek, Mariusz... We went to her house. It was pouring like from a barrel. It was dark.

Stasia could smell the rotting leaves on the forest floor, sweet and harsh, like blood. Her dress got wet and clung to her thighs making it difficult to walk. Twigs cracked underneath their shoes. They each found a large branch to use as a weapon. Marek slashed through the bushes, Jacek leaned on his like a walking stick. Mariusz pretended to be a witch flying on her broom. They laughed. Stasia held Marek's hand. It felt so good. He never let her hold his hand in public.

The witch's house was dark. She must have gone to bed. Her door was unlocked, like most houses in the village, so we could enter quietly. The doghouse was empty. The witch probably released the mutt to run with the village dogs. Every night after Mama tucks Stasia in, they call to her lulling her to sleep. Mama always says, Mother's love is greatest; then a dog's, then a sweetheart's.

We couldn't see anything. Stasia could hear the witch's breath in the corner like a pig with its throat slashed. We had a flashlight that Marek bought in the village store with our money. I sell eggs. Ten *groszy* per egg, Stasia smiles.

What happened next?

Someone walked into a table, and knocked something off. It crashed to the floor. The witch woke up and started screaming. In the flashes of light that bounced wildly around the room Stasia saw a mass of grey hair, and *Pani* Góraj's dark mouth with her one tooth sticking out like a potato in moist chernozem soil. Everyone was screaming. Someone pushed Stasia forward. She swung her branch.

What did you do? Where was Marek?

I don't know. It was dark like an oven, there was noise from our sticks hitting things, the screaming.

You must know what you did, at least, says Fatty.

Yes. No. I don't know. I hit. I dropped my branch and couldn't find it. My arms hurt. And then I saw Her.

Who?

Bozia. On the wall, over the bed. She was holding baby Jesus in her arms and crying. So *Pani* Góraj couldn't be a witch, you see. Because she had Bozia. My Mama has the same one. She keeps Her in the credenza drawer with the palms from Palm Sunday, and the communion wafer that we share at Christmas Eve.

What happened next?

Bozia punished us. I could feel her breath come in through the window. It made the sheers bulge out like Mama's apron over her stomach, and there was buzzing in the air, like altar bells. And then came the pain. I could feel it everywhere. My face, my eyes, my hands. Judgment day. We screamed and ran. Bozia chased after us.

And then?

I ran as fast as I could, but I was too slow and was left behind. Something else followed me. It bit me on my calf. It was a dog. Why would it bite me? Dogs love me. I cried. I couldn't see anything. I hit something. I thought I'd run into a tree. But it was Łukasz. I was so happy to see him. I thought I was lost.

Łukasz? I thought you said he wasn't there, said Fatty.

I don't know. Maybe he came to look for me. Maybe Mama had sent him. I hugged him. I held on to him like the board of last resort. He smelled sweet, like honey.

Pani Zuza crosses herself. Grasshopper shrugs. Fatty and circles his index finger around his temple.

Aha! Now we are getting somewhere, he says.

WOMEN

CICADA

The sofa feels so cold under Helena's hands that for a moment she wonders if she has wet herself. But then she realizes she is wearing a diaper. It's her last one—she will have to search the garbage pail, it could be days before her son comes home. The scream of the ambulance carrying Andrzej hits the window panes, bounces against the walls of the passageway leading from the courtyard to the street, and echoes faintly down *Aleja Niepodległości,* Independence Street. All is quiet again.

Helena hears sounds in silence. The sigh of water as it cools down in the kettle on the stove, the tiny bubbles bursting as the tea leaves sink to the bottom of her cup on the kitchen table, but there are no footsteps crunching the carpet fibers or slapping the linoleum. She has put Andrzej's slippers under his bed.

It must be noon. The sun warms her face. It's been gaining in intensity over the last few days. She heard buzzing in the air yesterday, when she went out on the balcony to pick up a pot of *bigos* she left out overnight. Andrzej's favourite soup. She was defrosting the fridge.

She can't breathe. Her heart races; she ran out of her drops months ago, and Andrzej keeps forgetting to refill her prescription. Her ears close, as if filled with earth. She is alone. Now even sounds have left her.

Please God, let somebody find me, Helena repeats in her mind. She doesn't pray often. She used to, but it never did any good. She waited until she was certain she could do nothing else, she needed a miracle, and then she prayed. It astonishes her that people keep on praying. Is that faith, or desperation?

A ping makes a sharp pain like a needle in her ear, and startles her. It's not the doorbell. Not a knock on the front door either—that makes a hollow, wooden sound, round like an open mouth. Ping! Here it is again. The glass balcony door. Blanka? No, she's been in the hospice for a few weeks now. Besides, they haven't spoken since Blanka's birthday a few years back, when Andrzej found Helena's card on their front door mat. Blanka had crossed out her age and written a smaller number with thick lines of red lipstick. *Czerwona Róża*, Blanka's favourite brand. Helena smelled it on the paper, and Andrzej laughed at them both. Too bad she's crazy, he sighed, she always had great booze at her parties!

It must be one of Blanka's sons out there, maybe Jarek. She heard him through the wall a few days ago, talking with Magda, but Andrzej called her crazy. They live in Canada now, he said. Of course she knew that, but maybe they came to visit Blanka. It's possible, isn't it?

The glass sound again. Helena pushes herself off the couch with her hands. Pain grabs at her knees, clamps down on her hips. She holds her breath. She can never get used to it. Old age. It's like the Little Mermaid, in pain at every step because she fell in love and became human. Andrzej loved that story. He asked her if she used to be a mermaid.

The floor creaks under her feet. She glides her hands over the chairs, the wood polished by the backs and hands that have touched it. The apartment feels larger every year.

Who is it? she asks when she opens the glass door. Cool

air blows into her face, ruffles her hair. She can feel it on her scalp. She hasn't seen her hair in so long. Maybe it's white now. My Goldilocks, Teofil used to say as he ran his hands through her curls.

Pani Szulska, it's me, Magda. Are you alright? Is Andrzej home? It *is* Jarek's wife. Her familiar, low voice makes Helena want to cry.

Andrzej is in the hospital, Helena says, and her legs melt like butter under her. She plunges into the dark cool air and lands softly against Magda's chest.

Gotcha! Magda says, and leads her slowly to the couch. Her hands are warm and dry. So much like Helena's mother's hands that for a moment Helena half expects her to pat her head and give her a toy.

What happened? Magda asks.

Three days ago Andrzej fell on the street. He—she can't say that he was so drunk that he lost consciousness. They all had made fun of Magda, the farm girl, who never took any alcohol, not even wine at mass.

He must have slipped on some ice, it still gets cold at night, doesn't it, Helena says. And maybe it was the truth. Maybe he fell because of the weather, the ice, a misstep. Or maybe somebody pushed him.

Some students found him, they wanted to call the ambulance but he took a cab home, Helena says, turning towards Magda's breath, a tiny whistle. Magda always had a large nose. But it was shapely. And her eyes were large and blue. She was beautiful. Helena wants to run her hands over her nose, her cheeks. To feel the flutter of her eyelashes like wings against her palms. How did Jarek get so lucky? Magda, three beautiful, successful children. He managed to emigrate across the iron curtain. Lives the American dream. In Canada, but still. What does he have that Andrzej doesn't? She and Blanka have always bragged about their sons. Jarek has dyslexia; he barely passed *Matura*, the matriculation exam, and had to repeat it before he was accepted to college.

Andrzej got top grades. He was smart, musical, popular. He studied architecture. She always told him he would be someone great, someone important. Blue blood flows in his veins. So many stunning girlfriends. And then Ewa, his last crush, got pregnant. They had to marry. He quit school. Paweł was born and the marriage went bad fast. Andrzej worked all day at construction, and came home late. He slept in the kitchen, so the baby wouldn't wake him. Ewa smoked on the balcony every day and ignored the crying. Magda had a baby then too, but she seemed happy. She'd walk across the joint balcony for playdates. She even breastfed Paweł because Ewa had no milk. While Ewa and Andrzej spent their nights arguing, Magda and Jarek made two more babies. When they moved finally into their own apartment from the government, Blanka regularly reported on how Jarek worked abroad, how the kids were all geniuses who took private piano and English lessons. All Helena could say was that Andrzej got divorced and didn't even want shared custody of Paweł. But he kept the apartment they had moved into just a year before they divorced.

So why is he in the hospital now? Asks Magda.

He got worse three days later, Helena says.

He'd seemed all right at first. Not like the time when he turned up at her door one night half naked, with a broken nose, a black eye and three cracked ribs. There were leaves in his hair and ligature marks on his wrists and ankles. He had drank his apartment away and she had to pay his debts with her savings.

This time a thump, something heavy and soft, fell on the rug in Andrzej's bedroom and woke her up. It was the middle of the night—the swishing of cars and buses was less frequent, and the hum of footsteps and voices, the constant background of her days, was gone. And the birds. They were sleeping. She heard Andrzej's footsteps; he dragged his feet with a swoosh over the carpet. Splat, splat, the soles of his feet struck the linoleum tiles in the kitchen. He was stumbling even though he wasn't drunk. A loud smack, like wet lips opening, of the rubber seal around the fridge door, a sigh of air, as he closed it. A pop and a hiss of a can of beer. Gurgling, and the low, guttural sound of Andrzej drinking. She could imagine his Adam's apple bobbing, swallowing poison. His neck long and alive, like an animal. His father's neck. She loved wrapping her hands around Teofil's neck when he arched above her. It was so long ago but she can still feel something pulsating inside her, blood rushing to her dead core. The feeling that only the young are supposed to have. Andrzej is nothing like his father, aside from his neck.

When she told Teofil that she was pregnant, he covered his face with his hands and collapsed on the floor. She didn't insist that he marry her, even before he explained that he couldn't jeopardize his law degree and the marriage his mother had arranged for him with a distant cousin. A *mésalliance* would devastate her. Helena let him go. Her own mother had died when she was only ten. She missed her all her life, promised herself never to abandon her son. At night she would come to his room to tuck in his blanket, but would stay there for hours looking at the sweaty curls on the back of his neck, and the long blond eyelashes. That is what she missed the most when she lost her sight. It happened gradually, after Andrzej moved his family into their own place. When Andrzej divorced and came back, Helena could no longer see him.

Teofil hanged himself the day before his wedding. She couldn't bear to think of his beautiful long neck, like a girl's, strung out on a rope. Bruised and broken. She was so angry. If he had lived maybe he would have met Andrzej one day, and everything would have been different.

Do you know when he is coming back, Helena? Magda asks.

No.

Later that night somebody shook her awake.

Ewa, Andrzej was saying, you whore, where have you been? I've been waiting all night.

Before she could answer Andrzej slapped her face. She pulled on the lamp switch cord before she slid off the sofa. There was a click and the fizz of the filament heating up in the light bulb. The smell of singing dust.

Oh my God, Mama, I'm so sorry, Andrzej cried, and tried to say something else, but it all became gibberish and he fell down on top of Helena, his face in her lap. His spit seeped through the thin cotton of her nightgown, and trickled down between her thighs. For a while his lips were moving, pinching and pulling on the soaked fabric, but she couldn't make out any words. What she could feel was his fear. She thought of the Christmas carp, flipping frantically on the cutting board before she jabbed the knife in its head. The crunch of the skull and the soft squirt of the brain.

She sat still until she heard the rumbling of the garbage truck, the metallic bang of the emptied garbage containers. The doors opening and closing in the building. Footsteps in the stairway, the squeak of the elevator doors, and the swish of its descent. She moved her legs so that he would wake up, but he was unconscious. She scrambled to the phone and called the ambulance.

Do you have anyone who can come and help you? Magda squeezes her shoulder. Helena looks up and shakes her head.

Then she remembers that a woman from social assistance comes to clean once a week. She is due tomorrow. Magda checks the food in the fridge, tells Helena where everything is and leaves. She has to visit Blanka in the hospice. She promises to come back soon.

A few days later Andrzej comes back. Helena is lifting a slice of rye with schmaltz to her mouth when she hears his footsteps, then the keys jingling outside the door. The scrape of metal when he puts the key into the lock. She smiles—he has aimed perfectly at the keyhole, which means his hands and eyes are steady. The lock clicks and the door yawns open; a draft swirls around her ankles.

Mama, I'm home, Andrzej calls out.

He embraces her and kisses her cheek. His skin feels smooth for the first time in so long. She touches his hair. It is still thick around the back of his head and ears but has that stiff, bristly feel of grey hair.

It seems funny that her son is an old man. She remembers when he turned three years old. She dressed him up in navy blue satin pants and matching shirt with a white lace collar she had crocheted herself. It was Palm Sunday—Teofil's parents were in church. When they emerged from the door she pushed Andrzej lightly towards them, and watched him as he climbed the steps. Teofil's mother ignored his raised chubby arms and walked towards their car without looking back. Helena grabbed him just as the vehicle pulled away. She resigned herself to raising her son alone. Later she heard that the communists took their property away and they emigrated to France.

It's good to have you back, son, she whispers in his hair.

No more drinking, no more lying. It was a wake-up call,

he says. Look, he opens the paper. She can hear the rustle of the pages and the fanned air lifts up her bangs briefly.

The stock market, I'm going to invest my retirement money.

Are you hungry? She pushes her plate towards him.

I already ate. I'm going to change, he says and goes to his room to put on his bathrobe.

When Andrzej gets his first retirement cheque he refuses to put it in their shared account. She knows he hasn't bought any stocks because he stopped talking about the stock market the day she heard him drag a case of beer into the apartment.

Mind your own business, he yells at her when she questions him. No wonder my father—she can hear him whisper to himself, but then the tea kettle whistles on the stove and she is grateful. She makes them both tea and they drink in silence.

She must have fallen asleep on the couch, because when she wakes up Andrzej is not home. She can't hear his snoring. It's very early in the morning, it's all quiet except the sparrows, and a cooing pigeon. She ran out of her eye drops and was afraid to tell him and then he had the accident. He needs to take her to a doctor's appointment today. She tries to get up to make coffee, but she falls off the sofa. Her walker, which she leans on to stand up, is gone. She walks into it on her way to the bathroom and hits her shin on the wire basket under the seat. It hurts, and the skin is sticky. She wipes her hands on the front of her nightgown over her thighs and then steadies herself against the wall on the way to the kitchen.

She is thirsty but her favourite mug and the tea kettle are missing. She gropes the counter space, lifts up the cereal boxes and the spice rack. She never mixes up the spices when she cooks; she sniffs each one before she shakes it over the pot. She loves cumin the most, Teofil smelled like that. The cutting board, the knife block, the paper towel on its upright plastic holder, the row of beer glasses—nothing seems to be right. It takes her an hour or longer, she has lost track of time, to find the kettle in the fridge, and her mug on the kitchen windowsill. When she finally feels the gritty texture of the clay under her fingers she cries. Andrzej made it at an art camp when he was seven. She lifts it to her face and inhales the scent of stale coffee and earth. This is not the first time she can't find things. Andrzej tells her she is going senile, but it only happens after they fight.

She is already dressed to go when Andrzej finally appears. He slams the door and stumbles inside. She can hear his shoulders scraping against the walls in the hallway, and the mirror and painting of poppies swinging on their nails. She won't be going anywhere today.

She can hear it, how drunk he is. It's a very peculiar sound, as if something inside his head is burning. Sizzling. The low hiss and splatter, like frying potato latkes. She leans back on the sofa. The air around her vibrates when he moves past. He drops into one of the dining-room chairs and bangs his head down on the table.

There is a knock on the balcony door. Andrzej pulls it open without getting off the chair or looking up, and then falls asleep. Magda has come to wash Blanka's nightgowns, she says, and asks, glancing at Andrzej, how Helena is doing.

Magda takes Helena to the hospital. Helena hates hospitals. She lost her babies there. She got married when Andrzej was six. She didn't love that man, but wanted Andrzej to have a father. He wanted his own children and got her pregnant four times, but she miscarried all of them. They lived with his mother, who had a bad temper and a heavy hand; she pushed Helena down the stairs after Helena had accidentally broken one of her heirloom plates. Fucking a count doesn't make you better than us, she shouted. She didn't know Helena was pregnant.

Helena never told her husband, she didn't want him to hate his mother. That backfired because her mother-in-law somehow convinced her son the second pregnancy was not from him. Helena went into labour several months too early when washing the kitchen floor. Her husband brought flowers to the hospital, but looked relieved he wouldn't have to raise two bastards. The next two pregnancies went away by themselves. She never told anyone. Then she lost her periods.

Don't cry, Magda says, and Helena feels her arm around her back. The doctor has everything on the computer, he will get you a new prescription, she says.

It's my heart, Helena says. My medicine ran out a month ago, but Andrzej...never had time to go with me. I need it more than the eye drops...

Helena, Magda says, we'll get it.

The doctor's hands are soft and dry, as if dusted with flour, velvety on her cheeks when he checks her eyes. He puts a few drops in each eye. They sting, but the pain feels good.

Andrzej is not a bad son, Magda, Helena says on a park bench outside the hospital. The seat is warm from the sun. The paint is peeling in round patches, the wood grain feels like tightly packed strands of hair.

It's the booze. With my pension I used to buy him a beer a day, to keep him happy. But now that he has his own retirement money...

What's that on your leg? Magda touches the spot Helena scraped against the walker.

It's nothing, she tucks her legs under the bench.

You could leave, Magda says.

I could leave? Helena repeats and turns her head towards Magda.

You could move to a nursing home. People can take care of you there. You would be comfortable and safe. Magda's fingers tighten on her wrists. Her breath smells like strawberry jam. Helena doesn't answer.

Sparrows are cheeping, crickets chitter in the grass, and a cicada chirps somewhere above her head.

She remembers the day when she and Andrzej found a broken toy bucket in a park. It was upside down so Andrzej turned it over, and said, bug, bug. Inside was a bright green cicada, with wide transparent wings and two eyes, like drops of blood, adorning the sides of its head. Attached to its back legs was a brown shell—its old skin. It must have been trapped under the bucket for days, who knows how long. When Helena carried it to a lilac bush and set it on a leaf, its wings tickled her palms like fluttering eyelids.

This is nice Magda, she says. It was nice to get away. From the sounds she'd rather not hear, from the beating of her failing heart.

GLAUCOMA

Magda bends over the bed and lets Blanka wrap her swollen arms around her. This is a fake hug; it's her mother-in-law's conscience at work. She's changed her will and now, half of the apartment belongs to Leon. When Magda had flown to Warsaw to take care of Blanka after the first stroke (Leon, who lives in a town less than an hour away, was too busy to help), she'd been promised that the apartment would be hers and Jarek's alone.

I hate this apartment as much as I hate my childhood, Leon said when Jarek asked his brother to chip in to buy it from the co-op for their mother. It's because of him we had to take a second mortgage on our condo in Toronto, Magda thinks, squeezing Blanka perhaps too hard. The old woman wheezes and coughs up phlegm.

Magda closes her eyes and chants Omm in her mind to release the negative energy. The sides of her neck and her shoulders spasm when she thinks of Leon. Easter is around the corner, and Leon told his mother that he can't come because he's working. Magda and Jarek both know that he is spending the holidays with his girlfriend. Not a muscle twitched on Blanka's face, hearing this on the phone. Instead she sent Leon loud smacking kisses before hanging up.

Alright Mama, Magda murmurs into a swollen lymph node below Blanka's right ear, we have to go now. She stands up and reaches for her coat.

Blanka rummages through the bag Magda gave her. Did you bring my chocolates? She pulls out a jar of prunes soaked in water, and an apple in a plastic bag. Did you scald it? Blanka asks. Raw skin gives me the runs. Blanka stuffs a kaiser bun with slices of smoked pork shoulder into her bedside cupboard, as though it was still the 1970s and the communist hospital cafeteria was as empty as department store shelves.

I need my chocolates! Blanka insists, otherwise they'll refuse to change my bedding, or make me beg for the bedpan. Or even worse, she whispers as she nods towards the hospice nurses' station, they'll spit in my food.

Magda fishes the bars of chocolate out of her coat pocket and hands them to Blanka, who doesn't realize that now, 25 years after the fall of communism, people expect better bribes. What Blanka thinks as valuable—coffee, chocolates, spirits, ham, exotic fruit—have been available for years.

In the hallway, a blowsy cleaning lady with crisp grey hair leans on her mop and waves her hand for Magda to come over.

Dear, can you bring cigarettes next time? she rasps.

No! Magda snaps. Do you want to die? My cousin is in chemo for lung cancer. She used to roll her own cigarettes. No filters.

The cleaning lady stares at her open-mouthed, and Magda's face feels hot. She turns away. Her hands shake so much she can't zip up her coat. Jarek pulls her by the elbow towards the exit.

Outside, the light is blinding. It's still cold, but the sun has that spring intensity, dandelion yellow. The soil is frozen into pale wrinkles. A robin lands on a bare branch in one of the large cement flower pots around the yard. Magda stretches her arms over her head. The energy of the sun enters her body. She presses her hands to the brittle grey bark of a tree growing in a square hole in the sidewalk, and hugs it.

Let's not go home yet, she says and looks into Jarek's face. It feels strange to be back in Poland and not feel at home. Everything has changed, everybody is older, sicker. They say Blanka is not going to last much longer; their son, Tomek, sent them one of his infrequent, one-sentence emails, which spurred them to fly over as soon as they could:

Grandma's lung not working, doc says it can be anytime.

Their phone conversations have not been any better; Tomek alarms them with his strange statements:

I don't know if I'm happy; Ala screams at me.
Why?
She says I can't even peel carrots.
What? Let me talk to her.
She is upset at you for saying she is getting too old to have kids.
What is she waiting for?
We are not ready, mom.
Are you looking for a job?
No.
When are you defending?
Don't know.

He used to call every two weeks before he met Ala. They got married quickly, he quit his job, and they moved back to Poland. Now, Magda has to call him, and he never answers anything, changes the topic, even lies. He is not happy, she knows that. She needs to talk to Ala.

When Ala asked about Blanka, Magda told her that Blanka feels loved, appreciated, and taken care of. We all need that and everything else is not important, she added, with a meaningful glance at Tomek.

Jarek, she says again, why don't we stay out for a while. Ala and Tomek could use some time alone. Magda doesn't tell him that the reason Ala drifts from room to room obsessively cleaning is to avoid conversation.

Jarek struggles with the buttons of his jacket but gives up when he can't close it over his bulging belly. They seem a bit tense, don't they? He stumbles over a hole in the sidewalk and bumps into Magda.

Well, where should we go? Łazienki Park? We could find a bench. My feet are hurting. He looks at her hopefully.

He dislikes the long walks Magda has been forcing him to take since his heart attack last summer. He would rather stay home and fiddle with his computer.

It's too cold to sit outside, Magda says. Let's go to Blanka's apartment. I need to wash her nighties anyway. She pulls a few green buds off the hedgerow branches scraping against her coat and inhales. She loves that sharp smell on her fingers when she pulls them apart.

And we can visit Andrzej, she adds, taking her husband's hand. He must miss having Blanka next door.

Magda, you know I don't like him. Jarek shrugs off her hand.

You aren't still mad? But you grew up together! I feel sorry for him—for his drinking. Taking care of his mother. He must be lonely.

She looks at Jarek. He is biting his lips, and there is a vertical line between his eyebrows. He can still be jealous, and she likes that about him, though Andrzej is of no interest to her.

When Magda left Jarek in Canada and came here to care for Blanka, Andrzej used to visit once every two weeks. He'd invite himself for dinner, and afterwards he played the piano. Magda insisted that Tomek stay in the room with them, because earlier, when she was pouring *biały barszcz* into his plate, Andrzej had kissed her hand. His lips were fleshy and wet and the shock of them on her skin made her drop the ladle. Hot soup spilled onto his lap and when he bent down to wipe his pants with a tea towel, the mangy hair around his bald spot made her feel sick.

We are not boys anymore. Don't expect me to be chatty. Jarek shakes his head and his upper lip lifts and gets caught over his long teeth. My ankle is hurting, I need to sit down.

Magda clasps his hand. The important thing is that they don't have to go back to her son's apartment yet. Ala doesn't even say good morning. She's offended. Offended by what? Being misunderstood, her son explained. What is there not to understand? She doesn't love her son. That is clear. Magda feels awkward there, but they can't stay in Blanka's apartment because it's not theirs. At least not yet.

A howling ambulance passes in front of Blanka's apartment building.

God, do you think it is *Pani* Szulska? See, it's fate that I wanted to go visit Andrzej. Something was telling me go, see him, Magda whispers and crosses herself. *Pani* Szulska is in her late 80s, and blind.

Maybe. You've always had a sixth sense about things, Jarek nods.

Magda smiles. Yes, she does have a gift. She feels it when people need her help. Once, she diagnosed her friend's son with mononucleosis after hearing briefly about the disease on the radio. Another time, her own mother confessed to years of abuse from her second husband; Magda had been right—she shouldn't have married him. And as soon as they arrived in Warsaw, Blanka's health improved. Her lungs cleared, she was alert; she lost weight, and was peppy. When she kept talking about a handsome young doctor who massaged Blanka's stomach and examined her stool, Magda took credit for her recovery. It's the positive energy I've been infusing her with, she thought.

The courtyard makes Magda nostalgic. She is expecting *Pan* Zdzisiek, who died years ago, to appear around the corner, pushing the soda fountain cart or watering the rose bushes. The tall poplar trees studded with crows' nests outside her kitchen window were recently cut down. And the kids' sandbox that Jarek and Andrzej had built in the corner is gone. She loves this building and the little one-bedroom apartment. Her children were all born during the seven years they'd lived there, until finally they got their own apartment in one of the new cement blocks on the outskirts of Warsaw.

The tiny old elevator with the inner wooden doors nestled in steel doors, still works. Magda used to take the wooden ones off to allow room for her stroller. She touches the small round 4th floor button. Her fingertips recognize its raised edges and the pressure it takes to push it. Andrzej still lives next door to Blanka, in his mother's apartment. His wife Ewa and Magda had been pregnant together, gave birth to their sons in the same hospital, a day apart. Now Andrzej's son has a baby daughter. Magda has stopped asking for a grandchild.

No one answers at Andrzej's door, so Magda decides to look into the apartment through the joint balcony door. Jarek stays inside to load up the washer with Blanka's dirty nightgowns. Magda stumbles past the empty, plastic flowerpots piled up against the wall. The railing is covered with pigeon droppings. Two cooking pots of *bigos* are out in the cold.

Magda presses her face to the grimy glass of Andrzej's balcony door. It feels cold. Tiny grains of dust stick to her forehead. Perched on the edge of an unmade sofa-bed is *Pani* Szulska. The light from the window strikes her long, hooked nose, and milky eyes. Her scalp shines pink through white, feathery hair. A half-plucked bird. She is mumbling something; her lips are moving. Her arms droop at her sides, hands resting on the bed along to each of her thighs. Her shapeless cotton nightgown makes her look like a girl.

She is alone. Alone in the dark. Magda knocks on the glass. *Pani* Szulska's mouth stops moving. She listens. Turns her face, gets up, and steps gingerly towards the balcony, arms stretched out in front of her, as if she were swimming. She grasps an armchair and pushes off it, steers by the table, hooks onto chairs, and docks for a moment at the handle of the glass door before she opens it.

Pani Szulska, it's me, Magda, Jarek's wife. Are you alright? Where's Andrzej? Magda wraps her arm around *Pani* Szulska's shoulders and leads her back to the bed.

I've been praying that someone comes to see me, Magda. *Pani* Szulska's voice trembles, and she drops onto the bed. Andrzej is in the hospital.

What happened? Magda sits beside her and holds her delicate hand in her lap.

He fell on the street a few days ago. He couldn't remember things, slurred his words, and got dizzy. I called the ambulance. *Pani* Szulska turns towards Magda, her cloudy irises skid, and settle somewhere above Magda's forehead.

My son drinks. With my pension I would buy him a beer or two a day, but now he gets his retirement cheques, and spends them on alcohol. I don't know what to do.

Don't worry, Magda says. I will talk to him. He has a granddaughter now, he needs to put money away for her education. When is he coming back?

I don't know.

Do you have anyone we can call?

Andrzej should have taken care of that before he was taken away. How can he leave his mother, blind and old, without any help? Maybe he was too sick to think about it. He is not a bad person.

A lady from social aid is coming tomorrow, says *Pani* Szulska.

Make sure you tell her what happened, that you are alone, Magda says. I will come back in a few days to check on you.

Blanka is having a fit.

I am your mother, you can't leave. He is a drunk! He is not family, she screams.

Magda has told her they are going to check if Andrzej is back.

Blanka is shaking and tries to get off the bed. Tears smear her mascara. Magda sits back down in the chair beside her and promises to stay a bit longer and come back in the evening. She remembers *Pani* Szulska on her bed, her hands at her sides, unmoving, like a holy statue. Their sons have neglected them both, but Blanka has Magda. *Pani* Szulska has no one.

Magda has always liked *Pani* Szulska, who babysat both her grandson Paweł and Tomek, because Blanka was unavailable—out dancing with her boyfriends when Magda needed help. But such is fate.

She looks at Blanka's bleeding cuticles. Every time they visit, Blanka picks at her skin and bites her fingernails, afraid they are going to ask about the will. But Blanka might die any day, so Magda is going to show Leon what a good son should be doing. She wants him to know they see Blanka every day, and that Magda hasn't visited anybody from her own family yet.

My God, how long has it been? Andrzej laughs and kisses Jarek on the cheeks. He is wearing a purple bathrobe with yellow flowers. The terry cloth is stringy and grey at the sleeves and on the collar where it crosses over his chest. Magda winces at the sour odor when he embraces her. She tries not to stare at his head, more bald now, the sunken cheeks.

You have not changed a bit Magda, as beautiful as ever, he says and smacks his lips. They look even thicker in his emaciated face. His eyes glide over her chest. She shudders.

I can't believe you are here! Ten years, he keeps saying as he moves the dining chair back for Magda. *Pani* Szulska is sitting on her bed, dressed and combed, smiling. When Magda comes over to hug her, *Pani* Szulska whispers in her ear excitedly: They detoxed him at the hospital! He said he won't touch the bottle ever again. My good boy is back.

So, how are you? Jarek asks, as he lifts a cup, and waits for Andrzej to pour the tea. Magda notices the even, unwavering stream and exchanges glances with Jarek.

I've learned my lesson, Andrzej laughs, and scratches the scabs and plum bruises on his forehead. I have some pictures to show you, he says and rubs his hands.

I'm so glad, Magda looks back at *Pani* Szulska and smiles. She wants to tell her, you see, everything is going to be well again. I promise you.

My granddaughter. So beautiful. She can sit up by herself already. Andrzej spreads the photos over the food stains on the linen tablecloth. Magda rubs the orange poppies on the fabric with her fingers. She remembers it from when *Pani* Szulska used to invite them all for tea on Saturday afternoons. It used to be special, now it's a rag.

Do you see Paweł often?

Not really, he is busy working. Odd jobs. He can barely support his wife and child. She's going back to work soon, but his mother-in-law is there every day helping out.

And you are retired now, you should open an account for the baby and put away money for her every month. You and your mom can manage comfortably on her pension. That's what we will do for our grandchildren.

Oh, are Tomek and his wife expecting? Andrzej asks.

They are thinking about it, Magda sighs. Education is the greatest gift you can give children, she says.

I don't know. That would be a lot of money, Andrzej stacks up the photos and slips them in his wallet like bills. I hardly ever see her. Paweł brings me pictures, you know, but never the baby.

She is only six months old, isn't she? When she is bigger, she will come over and play. She will love her grandpa, you will see. And her great-grandmother. She looks over her shoulder at *Pani* Szulska, who seems to have fallen asleep, her head rolled back against the back of the sofa, her sagging mouth half-open.

Andrzej needs a job, he needs to help his son, Magda thinks. She tells him how Jarek has started a consulting business, internet and computer safety, but Andrzej knows nothing about computers, neither does Paweł. Andrzej worked as a salesman, entertainer, musician. He has people skills, or rather, he used to have them. What could he do now?

Oh, I have a great idea! Magda slaps her hands down on the table. Do you know bee pollen?

Bee pollen? What about it?

People eat it.

No, really? Andrzej scratches the side of his nose.

Yes, it's very good for you. Has all the vitamins and microelements. It's like medicine, Magda says.

We eat it, Jarek says. You take a quarter of a teaspoon daily, not more because it is very powerful. Jarek takes a sip of tea.

Yes! You can make it and sell it. Magda beams.

How?

What do you mean how? Magda says. You raise bees, and take it from the hive. It's how they make honey. Paweł's wife is from Lithuania, right? I'm sure you can buy or rent some cheap land there, somewhere near a forest on a meadow, unpolluted. And you can build beehives. Collect the pollen, sell it, and *voilà*!

And there is a lot of money in that?

Sure. Who wouldn't want to eat bee pollen? Everybody is so health conscious these days. You'll have to advertise—

On the internet, says Jarek.

—but you can work out all that later, says Magda.

She can already see it all. The sunny meadow, the bees, just like when she was a little girl and her father kept bees in the orchard behind their farmhouse.

Well, I could talk to Paweł about it, if you think it is a good idea. Andrzej looks at Jarek.

Yes, do. It would be a great way to invest your money. Jarek reaches for the teapot, but it's empty. Only you know, once you have a business you must stay sober, not drink anymore.

Yes, yes, I know. Andrzej nods and looks at Magda. His eyes are still cornflower blue. He puts his hand on his chest, where the heart beats. I promise. He means it. She sees it in his eyes. He is going to be a changed man.

Magda, we should leave soon, we promised mother, Jarek pats her arm.

Oh, yes, I forgot! Magda starts. And then she feels it. That feeling she has about people who need her. She wraps her arms around Andrzej and hugs him. She can feel the energy passing from her into his worn body. Be well, she says in her mind, be well and happy.

Out on the balcony Magda feels faint. The world whirls around her and she grips the rail. The cold metal burns her skin.

Are you alright? Jarek grabs her arm.

I'm ok. I think I gave away all my energy and have nothing left. I will be fine. I just need to meditate.

Inside Blanka's apartment, Magda sits down cross-legged on the striped brown carpet, opens her palms to the sky. Jarek gives her a chocolate bar he has found in his coat pocket. She hasn't eaten anything since porridge for breakfast. After a few bites she feels much better.

When the laundry is finished, she goes out on the balcony to hang it to dry while Jarek watches TV. As she is fixing the last clothes pin on the line, Andrzej comes out on the balcony. His step is light, full of energy, his face bright. Such a change from an hour before.

I just had this amazing idea, he says. A gift for my granddaughter. With my retirement money I'm going to buy her a new stroller. One of these hi-tech ones that last forever!

Well, it is a good beginning, Magda says. It shows how he has started to transform, slowly but surely.

He leans closer. She steps back. She can smell it on his breath.

She can't believe she wasted her energy for nothing. Maybe he doesn't want to be helped.

Magda? Jarek calls from inside the apartment. Are you finished? Mom's going to be mad if we are late.

Yes, I'm coming, of course I am. She is doing so much better since I've taken care of her, she says to Andrzej. We have to hurry, I still need to make dinner for Tomek when we get home.

Andrzej leans over the railing and lights a cigarette. Magda winces at the smoke.

You will die from this, she wants to say. She watches the ashes fall off the tip and disappear somewhere down below, where she can no longer see, until Jarek's voice calls her back.

THE RUG

I slip off my shoes and wiggle my toes. Nine hours on the plane to see my son. The suitcase slips from my hand, thuds on the hallway tiles. The rug in the living room. It's the wrong colour. I remember the downtown store. The towers of colorful blankets. And on the back wall, the most beautiful rug I have ever seen—intricate blue pattern of leaves and branches. Turquoise spheres among them, like moons on an alien planet. The fibers were so soft. 100% wool.

We all kiss and hug. I drop into a chair. Tomek and Ala are finishing breakfast. On opposite ends of the couch. They have moved it to the other side of the rug. Luckily, no scratches on the hardwood. Is it possible the rug wasn't blue? Because it is red, fiery red. My eyes are burning. I feel a headache coming on.

Tomek looks so skinny. Is Ala feeding him right? He said he doesn't know if he is happy. When is he defending his thesis? Is he looking for a job? Is Ala pregnant?

I am here now.

I hate these surprise visits. Tomek, as always, forgot to tell me. I haven't slept all night, thinking about the weeks to come, the constant urgings to eat Magda's healthy delicious meals filling the already-bursting fridge, remarks on how thin Tomek is, how untidy the apartment is. Magda's infantile conversations with Tomek. You are not eating, are you feeling alright? Did you poop today? Do you have a fever? Magda will touch his forehead. Are you sweaty? Magda will stick her hand deep behind the collar of his shirt to check. You opened a window? Do you want to catch a cold? Put on a sweatshirt, it's drafty. Don't carry that, Ala can manage.

I should have realized I had married a child.

For two days I've been cleaning, washing windows in the chilly November air, ironing, folding, cooking because Tomek doesn't know how. I bet Magda will still complain I don't take care of the apartment, I don't take care of Tomek.

She had seemed so friendly. Make yourself at home, she had said when she unlocked the apartment. It smelled like paint and wood varnish. I kissed her. I just got a job in Warsaw and couldn't afford to rent. She hardly knew me, we had met twice before, once in Toronto, the summer after Tomek and I met, and the second time at the wedding in Warsaw. And yet she trusted me to live there alone before Tomek came back from the US. I thought I was going to have a mother again. I tried to please her. All the instructions. Mind the hardwood! If you decide to rearrange the furniture, be careful. In the bedroom Magda rubbed the doorframe. This used to be Tomek's, she said, but would make a perfect baby room. She stared at my hips.

I really don't understand why you don't want to live in Canada, Ala. Everybody I know wants to emigrate. She pressed the key in my hand so hard it hurt.

A sheer blouse drapes the armrest smelling strongly of perfume. I lift it up in my fingertips and let if fall on the floor. My apartment, which I have renovated with money pinched from Jarek's salary; the apartment where my children grew up; the apartment I miraculously managed to buy from the co-op before we emigrated, in case we had to return to Poland—my precious apartment looks like a slum! Piles of shoes and clothes everywhere, spilling out of plastic storage containers (why haven't they bought wardrobes?), several cheap-looking chairs stacked together, tables that don't match, two TVs.

    What is all this junk?

    Ala sips a large cup of tea looking somewhere above my head each time she swallows. Tomek cradles a bowl of cereal in his lap, spoon in his fist, a childhood habit. The only sound—crunching cornflakes.

    They are Gosia's things, Tomek says. Ala chokes on her tea and coughs.

    Can't she put them in the basement? The apartment looks like a pawnshop, I stare at Ala, she studies a crack in her cup.

    She broke up with her boyfriend, and can't afford her own place, Ala says and looks at Tomek like she is waiting for something.

    She lives here? I ask. I remember the boyfriend from the wedding. He owned a used furniture store. He avoided my eyes and kept ogling the bridesmaids.

    I thought Tomek asked you, Ala says and stirs her tea. The spoon rattles in the cup.

    He didn't. I run my foot over a stiff patch of fibers. Is that a stain?

    You told us to feel at home.

    Don't be ridiculous. You can live in my apartment, sit on my sofa, cook in my kitchen, yes, but you do not invite strangers to live here!

    Gosia is family, Mama, Tomek says and puts down his bowl on the side table. He wipes his mouth with the back of his hand.

Gosia does have a lot of issues, but she's my sister. Who can blame her for dropping out of school and leaving home? I wish I had this kind of courage. She would stay away as long as dad was drinking and beating us or until mom left. Which never happened. I somehow finished law school, and I will support her as long as I can, through all of her failed relationships and crazy money-making schemes.

Not my family, I say and notice Ala pinches her lips together. And you live here in this threesome? What kind of marriage is that?

I want to grab Ala's skinny arms and shake her. Tomek is a perfect son. My daughters fought with me over boys, school, clothes, food. Tomek visited his grandmother in the hospice every day, like I asked, even massaged her knees. He makes sure I cook organic. Ala and Gosia probably gossip and laugh together while Tomek sits alone in front of his computer. No wonder Ala isn't pregnant.

I lived with my mother-in-law for seven years while a new apartment block was constructed in the slow communist economy. We bought her movie tickets and health spa trips when we wanted to be alone. Three kids within four years!

What is Ala waiting for? She is not young. Does she even appreciate that she is living rent-free? Without Tomek she would have to move back to the farm. No wonder she married quickly—a Canadian with an apartment in Warsaw. A guy who'd given up his job in Silicon Valley, for her!

So what if he still doesn't have a job in Poland. Ala makes enough. If she had helped him, he would have graduated his Master's already. I used to make him do his homework. He is a genius, easily distracted like his father. I had to convince him to ask for a raise, and to take his engineering certificate exam in Canada. That is what wives are for. Ala must not love him. I never hear her praise him. She called me once, to say he took a

whole day to peel and dice identical-sized potato cubes for soup.
    It's not neurosurgery, Ala said.
    I never ask my husband to cook, I told her. It's a matter of pride. You should have shown Tomek how to do it, not scream at him. Most men would simply refuse to cook, I said. She never called again.
    At least they can divorce. A government license means nothing. They are living in sin, but now I see it was God's will.
    Gosia has to move out and take her junk. I give you three days.
    But she has no place to live! cries Ala.
    She can move back in with your parents.
    With my father, Ala puts her teacup down. The spoon pings against porcelain but I feel it in my temples.

It's amazing how one person's suffering is forgettable for others. I miss my mom so much. Advanced breast cancer with bone metastases. We couldn't do anything. Dad sits at the grave every day, whispering kind words he never used when she was alive. Gosia still refuses to visit. She will never forgive him for the attack with a knife. Reks, who was off the chain at the time, bit his arm. I go every weekend to help out on the farm and play with the dog.

    I can't stay still. The rug fibers crunch under my feet. They are synthetic!
    Tomek puts his arm around Ala's waist, but she shakes it off. Her eyes are the colour of cement.
    Do you love my son?
    What? I don't—
    You stole my rug!
    Ala's mouth opens so wide I can see the black hole down her throat.

I don't know what a loving marriage is. Of course Tomek is staring at the floor. Not at the rug, but at the floor we have been so careful not to scratch. He will never stand up to his mother. He is not a man.

At Sylvia's Christmas party, a few years back, Sylvia was showing off the new sauna her husband installed in the extension. She asked Tomek what he did. He shrugged his shoulders and said, Nothing. I wanted to hide. I laughed quickly and slapped his arm. He is working on his Master's in computer science, I said. I didn't say it had been five years now, he had seen his supervisor only once. When my friends talk about their babies, new houses, trips all over Europe, I nod and smile with my jaw so tight I feel like I'm going to choke on my teeth. I never thought we would end up like this.

My cousin convinced me to go on a blind date. A Polish-Canadian computer programmer. He was young, tall, good-looking. Beige dress pants and pink golf shirt—his mother must dress him, I thought—good. He stared at my breasts He was weird from the beginning, but I thought—eccentric. Did he know that retirees and the homeless eat at milk bars, the relics from the Communist era? I was glad none of my friends saw us. He later said he felt nostalgic.

He was without swagger or smooth talk, naïve and socially awkward, as if he were from another planet. But he won me over when he said he was looking for a wife. What man says that? I thought he was a good one.

Gosia said, he is perfect for you! I called to ask him for a second date. Once, when he bent to tie his eternally undone shoelaces, a paper fell out of his pocket. I grabbed it without him noticing. My name was on a list of six women with times and dates.

The night before he went back to Canada, he wanted to make love (he didn't say sex. I liked that). I said yes if he promised to marry

me. I was half-joking. I was sure he was a virgin too, and I didn't want to wait for the right guy any longer. He twisted my nipples like they were bottle caps, and rubbed the outside of my vagina as if it was my clit. We both had a lot to learn. I was in love.
   I didn't know about the hypochondria. All the cashiers at the grocery store know Tomek by name, asking about additives in every product. I put my favourite red sandals in our tiny basement storage locker, and Tomek threw them out fearing lung cancer from asbestos stored in an adjacent space. I didn't speak to him for three days.

I remember the tag on the underside of the rug, in one of the corners. The tag I read in the store several times. 100% wool—for that price, a bargain. When it was delivered, I walked on it barefoot for days.

What is she doing now? She's on her knees, crawling along the edge of the rug, kneading it like a cat, checking the underside of each corner.
   This can't be happening.

   Here! I yell pulling the tag off. There is a staccato of torn stitches. I show it to Ala.
   What is that?
   Proof!
   80% propylene, 20% cotton, Ala reads.
   Exactly. When I bought this rug, it was a 100% wool.
   I don't know.
   You don't? I'm shaking. I need to sit down. How can she still deny it?
   This is the same rug, Ala says, her elbow swipes the teacup off the end table. It falls on the carpet; the spoon bounces on the hardwood floor. The teabag lands like a turd at my feet.

I'm ignoring it. It's not my rug that is getting stained.

What happened to the clothes I left here? And the new phone? I ask. There are things missing in this house, yet it's full of random pieces of furniture. Stolen no doubt.

Ala looks at Tomek cleaning his glasses with the bottom edge of his T-shirt. We gave them to charity. You are here so rarely, she says.

We donated them to a store downtown, he says and puts his glasses back on his nose. Ala leans back against the couch.

He is lying to protect her. I can't be angry at him for being loyal to his wife. But he is wrong. My best clothes left behind to make room for gifts for the family. You didn't think to ask me?

We didn't think you wanted them! Ala's voice shakes. She glares at Tomek. Tomek said we could do whatever we wanted with them.

No I didn't, Tomek turns to Ala, wide-awake eyes for the first time.

Yes, you did!

I don't remember.

Tomek! Ala gets up. Her face and neck covered with red splotches.

Tomek rubs his nose where the glasses pinch. Maybe I forgot to ask, he says slowly. Or maybe you forgot that we asked you, Mama?

Son, would I agree to have my clothes thrown out of my own apartment? Would I agree to a stranger living here, and storing this stolen property? And what about my phone?

You think I stole your clothes, your phone, your rug? Hoping you wouldn't notice? All to make a few *złoty*?

Exactly! I say. She can pull wool over my son's eyes, but not mine.

Ala leaves, slams the bedroom door.

I can still hear them, even with the pillow over my head. Maybe I should just pack up and leave. Leave Tomek, his crazy family, the apartment. Only where would I stay? What if I won't find anyone? I'm 40 years old. I hate living alone.

I am a part of this family. I do the housework, the cleaning, the cooking, the laundry. I pay the utilities and support him. If I leave, Magda wins. I will stay in this apartment. I will mark my presence. Starting with Tomek.

    What phone Mama?
    The one I bought last time.
    Oh, that. Ala gave it to her father because his broke, said Tomek.
    She took my phone and gave it away?
    We don't need it and he does, Mama! Why are you attacking Ala? All she wants to do is help her family.
    You are naïve, Tomek. She wouldn't be with you if you didn't have this apartment. Don't you see that? She asked you to put her name on the deed? Remember? If I had allowed that, you would be on the street now, and she and Gosia would be living here!

It's been seven years. Still, no orgasm. Tomek tells me I need to shower first. He is the one who stinks—no deodorant—the chemicals cause cancer, he says. I don't wear makeup anymore. He says it makes me look cheap.

    Once I embraced him from behind. He flinched. He apologized and cried too, but his reaction never changed. I stopped trying.

    No, Mama, that was my idea, not hers.

I don't believe you. She convinced you it was your idea.

She is not like that Mama. Ala is not a thief. It's impossible. She is a lawyer, she would lose her job.

Tomek, I gave her everything, this apartment to live in, money for her father's new fence and her sister's window-display course. I gave her my son! And she just barks or mumbles when I try to talk to her. Son, what kind of wife spends every weekend with her dad and her dog, instead her husband?

Maybe the men in the store lied to you about the carpet. Maybe they delivered the wrong one?

Tomek, do you think I made up all this stuff?

Mama, this is insane. You can't accuse people. If both sides were presented in court, you would lose. Wait! I have evidence. Pictures from the apartment before Ala and I moved in.

So he thinks this is insane! I wipe my face. A photograph! Magda is forever taking pictures, posing. Magda in her Toronto condo, smiling among stiff, plastic flowers.

I'm telling you, that rug's going to be blue.

Tomek searches his computer files. I sit on the rug wishing I could make it change its colour. This red is so ugly, Tomek. Why would I buy an ugly rug?

Look!

There is a picture of me sitting cross-legged—forefinger and thumb forming a circle. Beneath me, the red rug.

It can't be true! What date was this taken?

Tomek points to the numbers on the screen. A few days after I gave Ala the keys, before Tomek moved in.

Ala replaced the rug before the picture was taken!

But Mama, you look happy! Wouldn't you have noticed the rug?

She photoshopped the picture!
She will admit to what she did. Tomek will come back to Toronto.

Magda outside the apartment, among the trees, which have grown so much during the last twenty years! Magda at the old kitchen table, still in pretty good condition, and keep it that way, keep that in mind, Ala! Proud Magda in the newly renovated bathroom, covered in ugly, pink tiles, even the ceiling. Magda with her arm around Tomek, gazing at his face.
A photograph will straighten her out! Magda will apologize!

MUSE

Basia braced herself as she neared the door. She fought with her umbrella and staggered, unused to her body. She saw herself through the eyes of the bus driver, an overweight woman with a round, childish face, her sack of a body hovering midstep. Her knee almost buckled, but she gripped the rail and hoisted herself in.

Basia looked around for a seat. Her gaze snagged on the eyes of a girl, a thin blanket covering her shoulders and chest. From the bulge it was obvious she was holding a baby. A teenage mother, unmarried—Basia gave her a fake smile. The bus started, and Basia reeled back, dropping into the closest seat, behind the girl. It was a safer choice than across the aisle, next to the man with the horse-face and a stained jogging suit.

The girl stared at Basia's protruding stomach, so Basia swung her book-filled shoulder bag in front of it. The girl turned her pale, freckled face towards Basia:

He's just four weeks old, but weighs 14 pounds. When he was born, he was ten pounds! I've never had such a large baby before. It still feels strange to hold him.

Really? Basia had no idea of the average weight of a newborn. She was afraid the girl might ask if she was pregnant. Basia considered a lie this time.

When are you due? a young woman holding a baby asked the plus-size heroine (note: name—Wilma?), *and fixed her gaze on Wilma's stomach. Wilma panicked. What month did she look? Third? She could talk about baby names.* Basia had several picked out. Maia or Yana for a girl, and Charles or Matthew for a boy. She would like a girl first. When could one know a baby's gender?

I'm in my fifth month. We don't want to know the sex, Wilma stuttered.

Basia wasn't a good liar.

An alternate scene:

When are you due? the girl stared hungrily at Wilma's bulging stomach.

Um, I'm not pregnant, it's—

Oh, I'm so sorry, the girl grimaced and reddened—no—took on the colour of a rare steak.

—it's my medication, Wilma whispered, her smile turtleneck-tight across her face. The drugs gave her a belly, stretch marks and all. The medical terminology: a moon face and a buffalo hump.

The girl nodded, thinking Wilma a greedy pig. (Point of view? An omniscient narrator? Out of favour these days, like God).

Basia wished she were reading, an excuse not to talk. She pressed the book bag to her chest. What had the girl meant when she said she hadn't a baby this big? Did she have others? She couldn't be more than 18. Tank top and camouflage cargo pants, lean body of a child, face fresh as a new page. No hint of dark circles under her round eyes. She should be at school passing notes behind the teacher's back.

Can I see him? Basia blurted out. The mother hesitated— Basia didn't expect that from someone so talkative. The girl lifted the edge of the sheet from her shoulder. Basia leaned in. The girl was breastfeeding. Basia blushed, too embarrassed to look more carefully. The soft roundness of cheek, a tiny nose pressed against his mother's breast, his little throat working like a pump. Even if she could have a baby (her husband had agreed to wait for her condition to stabilize), Basia wouldn't be able to breastfeed because of her medication.

He is beautiful, Basia said, unsure whether she was lying or not.

I can't get used to him, the girl said. My first was much smaller... I have a five-year-old son. He is with his father, she explained. Basia nodded, subtracting five from 18. No wedding ring. Basia didn't wear hers either (her fingers had grown too fat and she hadn't bothered to resize it because she was still gaining), so she couldn't be too critical. Why would that change anything? Would the father care more if they were married? Who said marriage meant stability?

Is his father a big man? Basia asked, as she tried to overcome her shock.

I guess so. If he ate more he would be quite stocky. He's over six feet tall, the girl finished feeding the baby, and held him against her shoulder to burp him. He raised his head, and looked vaguely at Basia, his eyes shallow like puddles.

I had a baby girl, a miscarriage, when I was 14, she added. Maybe I can't carry girls. I was so upset. The father said not to worry, we would have many more babies.

Basia saw the scene: the girl crying on his shoulder, her blueberry lipstick on his shirt. When she wiped her face, her black fingernails looked like bruises.

My God, this girl was pregnant at 14. Now has two children and a mucky history. You couldn't read it in her face. Had she graduated from high school? What kind of life did she have?

Her name was Jane. She'd dropped out after her baby was born. She worked as a cashier at a small grocery store. She wore a nylon shirt too tight for her post-partum body, her sweat and leaky breasts made her itch. Her bitten fingernails scraped against the keys as if she were digging. No. Her fingers moved over the register keys as if it were a typewriter writing a steamy romance that ended with a wedding. Each of Jane's days included a long bus ride home, a three-storey walk-up—no, better yet—a basement apartment without a laundry room, where her mother watched soaps and reminded Jane of her failings in order to forget her own.

*Yet Jane was happy. Ever since she was a little girl playing with dolls, all she wanted was to be a mother. She felt fulfilled. Each time she looked at the baby she felt a warm glow...*No, that's garbage. Basia looked at the girl.

Jane ignored the screaming baby and went to the kitchen to make mac and cheese. The last box was empty. Damn it mom, you could've left me some. Jane threw the container at the table, where her mother sat, staring at the plastic ashtray in front of her. She took a drag of her cigarette and said: Your kid's crying.

Jane shrugged. She was sure the baby hated her as much as she hated her mother—he screamed harder when she picked him up.

There was no such thing as being able to carry only boys or girls, Basia was sure of that. She had a graduate degree in physiology. The girl had probably been too young. Or there had been a genetic problem with the fetus.

Basia sighed. She would still be working in the lab if it weren't for her health. It got so bad she couldn't lift a test tube or press down a syringe plunger. *Myasthenia gravis*—the body attacking itself, signals not getting from nerves to muscles. As if she had a brain but no body.

When she left work she cried. Even her medication didn't allow her to continue. Basia's appearance changed so that her friends didn't recognize her. She avoided those who didn't know she was sick. Her new life confused her. Its cruel randomness terrified her.

Her husband supported her and she spent her time resting, reading constantly. She'd always loved literature—critically acclaimed authors, the classics, post-modernists. She had taken English at university, even tried to write, but good books gave her writer's block. Sometimes she wished her favourite authors would die, so she wouldn't have to endure each new novel—the artistry she could never achieve. She read so quickly, with such hunger that she had no time to think about what she'd read. If reading were drinking, she was merely rinsing her mouth.

Books lay scattered on the floor, in piles on the coffee table, in uneven stacks beside her bed, spilled over into the bathrooms. Her walls of books closed in on her. She couldn't keep up with the list in her notebook.

She read till her eyes hurt and her head ached. She read instead of cleaning, or shopping, or talking to neighbours, or sleeping beside her snoring husband.

The mother lifted the baby over her shoulder. He grimaced, and spittle dripped on the girl's face. Basia pressed back against her seat. Babies are a Pandora's box of germs to the immunocompromised. Hand, foot and mouth disease, pneumonia, meningitis, gastroenteritis, death.

He has such beautiful blue eyes, Basia said. What she really wanted to say was How old are you?

The girl smiled. His father's eyes, she said. We've just came from him—in Hawrelak Park. We love the river.

Oh yes, Basia had no idea where that was. She didn't know Edmonton that well. She left the house rarely, to the doctor or the bookstore.

He is such a proud daddy, walking around with his son in the baby carrier. Now it hangs too low and hurts my back, the girl fiddled with the plastic clasps on the straps, trying to shorten them. The baby started to cry. The girl turned away from Basia, holding him to her chest, patting his round back. Basia wondered how many fathers there were.

Jane broke up with the father of her first child when he went away to college. His parents took the baby. She didn't fight them; she was tired of his constant wailing and missed her friends and parties. She saw the child occasionally, timing her visits to avoid the father. Soon she met Erik and fell in love with his quiet voice and tattooed arms. When a plus sign appeared on the stick again, she couldn't believe it.

Basia felt sorry for her. She wanted to touch her face, reflected in the rain-spattered glass of the bus window like it was under water. Her oily, dirty-blond hair gathered back in a pony-tail, revealed a sturdy, triangular face, large mouth and a wide, flat nose. Her voice had sounded clear and bright when she mentioned her miscarriage.

Basia remembered how, as a child, she was drawn to pools of water on soccer fields after thunderstorms. But when she looked at the ripples she felt dizzy and couldn't breathe thinking she might fall in. The girl was probably one of those children who just plunged into water.

Basia's life was careful. She graduated from university, then dated her husband for several years, before moving in together. They always used condoms even though she was on the pill. They got engaged after three years, and a year after were married. Ten years on, Basia felt she'd known her husband forever. The only thing she didn't plan was her illness.

The girl bent over the child. A plastic bottle of formula rolled on the floor. Didn't she know about carcinogens? The girl picked it up, licked the nipple and put in the baby's mouth. Basia cringed. The baby kicked his bare feet like tiny fish. Tiny, purple, cold fish.

What's in your bag? the girl asked. It looks heavy.

Oh, just books, Basia didn't want to bore her. She probably read only fashion magazines.

Really? We just finished Anna Karenina in my lit course. I like Tolstoy, but Dostoyevsky has a terrible style, don't you think?

Jane hated reading and looked with distaste at the fat woman beside her. She had just pulled a book out of her bag, held it in one of her plump hands, and raised a chocolate bar to her mouth with the other. The fat on her lower stomach hung like a rolled-up carpet between her thighs. God, I hope I'll never be like her, Jane thought and pinched the small mound of fat around her waist.

The girl kissed her baby, and held him with such ease. It was clear she was used to holding babies, that she loved him. Maybe she'd even planned to have him, and her other children as well. Was it possible she knew what she wanted?

Basia pulled her book bag to her side and stood up. She decided to get off at the next stop, to walk a little. Out the window, flowers in the front yards of houses seemed to explode and die against the walls like fireworks.

BYPASS

I will never give him a divorce, Jolanta thinks as she marches down the grey hospital hallway, her heels hammering each shiny tile, the yellow CAUTION sign splayed open on the wet floor like a jaw. But he will pay for this betrayal.

When Leon disappeared weeks ago she thought he was punishing her after one of their fights, she didn't even remember what about. Probably money. He got fired for drinking on the job, again. He would be back soon, she thought, when his friends were done with his sarcasm and lordliness, the empty beer bottles and crusty pizza boxes. Or when he tires of his mother's nagging. He would come back like nothing happened and she would play along, because neither would say sorry or pretend to be sorry to smooth things over. Who else would put up with him?

He called her cell. She was eating a hot dog at her booth, staring through the falling rain at the Palace of Culture and Science, the post-war gift from the Soviets. Leon disparaged its ugly architecture, the palace of traitors, he called it. With them came freedom, but they overstayed their welcome. She'd learned to love it: it was impressive despite its imperfections. Almost beautiful, with its edges dissolving like watercolour into the misty rain, the awnings of the market stalls around it like colorful stacks of banknotes. Now, decades later, it was an undeniable emblem of Warsaw, impervious to changing political and social climates. The phone wouldn't stop ringing. She didn't recognize the number, but took the call anyway.

I want a divorce, Leon's smoker's voice grated in her ear.

When are you coming home? she asked, gulping down a chunk of hotdog. I miss—she wanted to add, but the meat had stubbornly lodged itself in her throat. She coughed hard, and tears burned her eyes.

I'm coming to get my things, he said.

I won't give you one, she finally swallowed. I love you.

You disgust me, Leon whispered into the phone. Was someone there with him? She thought she heard a woman's voice.

You are just saying it, you love me I know it, Jolanta took another bite, and licked the ketchup off her fingers.

I don't love you, he said, louder this time.

I don't believe you. And anyway, we had a church wedding. I couldn't divorce you even if I wanted. It's a sin.

Since when do you believe in God?

We had our kids baptized, remember? she snapped. She didn't go to church, but who did? Most people went at Christmas and Easter; perfect Catholics. But she saw them daydreaming through the sermon, leaving before the closing hymns.

I will never divorce you. I will wait for you. You always come back. No one else loves you like I do, she shouted into the phone. But he had already hung up.

The first time they met she was standing in the vestibule of the PKP train car, Arek sat on one of the suitcases at her feet, pushing his toy car under the handle as if an underpass, growling engine sounds. She had finally left her boyfriend for good.

The skin around her right eye was still yellow, and she had covered the plum-coloured tracks on her neck with a bright blue scarf. It was so crowded that she didn't have to hold on to anything, just let her body lean against others in the rhythmic rocking of the car. She must have dozed off, and when she woke up she saw his grey eyes, the square jaw. He spoke to her in French. She didn't understand a word; it sounded like a brook, wet and sparkling. When he asked if she was from Paris, she blushed and yanked off her puffy *frotté* hair tie when he wasn't looking. Their hands touched as he grabbed her suitcase; he found an empty compartment and took her there. Neither of them had a ticket, they confessed to each other later and laughed.

She waited for Leon and thought of his phone call. She'd checked the number online. It belonged to a Zofia Witak. So now she knew. It really didn't matter. He always fell for weak, needy women, easily impressed by his drunken erudition. Yes, he could turn the charm on, the civil engineer, the architect, he called himself, but never mentioned he was unemployed. The last one was a university undergrad, 20 years his junior. She left him when she realized his socks stank and his misogyny was greater than her daddy's. Jolanta got him back. She always did. Przemek and Ola. Pregnancy was his breaking point. He married his first wife because she was pregnant. She divorced him when she lost the baby. Now she was happily married with three kids. Jolanta often wondered whether his ex ever felt grateful for the miscarriage. When Ola was born he came back, staggered at the threshold of her hospital room with a bunch of wilted lilacs. His only daughter, he cried and hugged them both. On the way home from the hospital she noticed the decimated lilac bushes by the emergency entrance. At home he told Jolanta his mother had changed her mind about his abortion when her legs were already spread in the stirrups. He never forgave her for not wanting him. Jolanta never told him about hers. But when Polish women skipped work on Black Monday to protest the medieval abortion bill, she closed up her stall, put on her sexiest tight black jeans and joined them on the streets. Leon disappeared for several days after he found out.

    She couldn't let him move his things out. She said to him, when they were newlyweds, what's yours is mine, and what's mine is also mine. They had laughed at that so much. How can she get him back this time? She is in menopause. She could pray for a miracle but she changed the lock instead. He can have the spare key when he moves back in. But she isn't as confident anymore. He never asked for a divorce before. Not for a woman. It has to be something serious.

    She fingers the new key now, at the door to the recovery room, it feels cold, even though it's midsummer. She is so hot her breasts, stiff as armor in her new brassiere, are slippery with sweat. She sucks in her belly and opens the door.

    Leon is lying under a white sheet, his bed against a white wall. An IV bag like a transparent boxing glove hangs over his square head. The tube coils down and disappears in the bandage on his heavily veined arm. His large hand, the dark hair above his wrist. Clutching the handle of her suitcase that night on the train. He never hit her. He didn't recoil, like other men, when she told him Arek was her son and that she wasn't married. His mother did, later on, but he didn't care. She loved him for that. They shared a bottle of vodka, made great money-making schemes and had quick sex in the train bathroom while Arek slept snuggled against her coat in the compartment. It was Leon who got her into the used clothing trade when she told him she had friends in Turkey. His mind was so quick. So sophisticated. She could listen to him for hours.

He looks yellowish, and somehow thinner. Younger. Not like a man who just had a double-bypass surgery. As she enters, he puts down the open pages of *Biznes Warszawski* on the blanket on his lap. The newspaper flutters and rustles, as if about to take off, but his voice sounds steady, heavy with distaste.

Oh, it's you, he says with an odd smirk on his face.

Jolanta looks around the room. A painfully thin, tall woman is sitting in a chair in the corner, knitting. She must be in her mid forties. Who knits at that age? So, fifteen years younger than him. Well. She moves towards Jolanta. Jolanta turns away, bends down to kiss Leon. She will not give him the satisfaction, she will not be the typical jealous wife. He jerks his head away, her kiss lands on his ear. Zofia stands at the foot of the bed, Jolanta sees from the corner of her eye. Busty. Short skirt exactly like the ones at her stall. Jolanta might even have sold it to her.

Zofia finally turns and gathers her knitting. I will be back in half an hour, sweetie, she says. Do you want anything from the cafeteria? she asks from the doorway.

Beer? Leon says and sends her one of his charming smiles. His teeth flash ghostly white in his tawny face.

Jolanta mocks her words with a silent movement of her lips and rolls her eyes. Sweetie?

Leon notices and shrugs his wide shoulders. Well? he grumbles, she can see the corners of his lips twitching.

She moves Zofia's chair to the bed. It's warm. She winces. It always disgusts her, someone else's body heat, from some smelly rear end. It's worse than sitting on a public toilet, a toilet can be cleaned. She puts her purse in her lap and leans towards Leon. Up close, his skin doesn't seem yellow at all. The whites of his eyes flash like hardboiled eggs. He probably hasn't had a drink since the attack. He is tanned! Who is he preening himself for? Zofia? No wonder he had a coronary—probably exerted himself in some gym or sauna. Or Zofia's bed. Jolanta squeezes her key hard, the metal bites into her palm. She relaxes her hold.

I came as soon as I heard, she says.

And the kids? When are they coming? He looks into her face, she can feel his gaze slide to her bust. Then back up. His jaw muscles moving as if collecting spit. Do they even know? he asks, sitting up. His hair, whatever is left, is completely white. People don't go grey overnight, it's a silly superstition. She wants to touch the bloodied bandage in the middle of his chest.

They are coming, I called them right away, Jolanta says. I tell them everything that concerns our family. She tries to catch his eye. *I don't have any secrets*, she says.

She called Arek first. He was on his cell, picking the kids up from school. She could hear them playing in the background.

His heart? I didn't know he had one, Arek said.

Don't say that, she said. He gave you his name.

Well, that's all he did. I was everything else, the cleaning lady, the nanny, the scapegoat, but never his son, Arek whispered angrily, probably not wanting the kids to hear. He paused. Is he ok, Mom?

Yes, I think so.

You think so? Arek asked. You haven't been to see him yet?

She was locking up the cash register.

I will be there tomorrow, he said. I can't today, need to take the kids to a soccer game, and Ania is working late at the lab.

Ola was on holidays in Gdansk. It was a bad connection. I'm so sorry mom, are you ok? she asked. She said she would come by as soon as they were back, the kids were having such a great time she didn't want to spoil it for them. Everything is so expensive here, she added. For all the tourists, I guess. They come from all over Europe, she said. It's because Poland is so safe. No terrorists or refugees, you know, mom.

Jolanta sighed. It amazed her how it was so easy for Ola to forget that her ancestors were refugees from Ukraine.

She couldn't get hold of Przemek. He had been out with some friends for a few days. First mountain climbing, after he begged her for money for some equipment, and she gave in because she worried for his safety, then the Patriot March. She saw them on TV, the vaguely fascist symbols, the columns of self-righteous young men with faces as pale and blunt as pigs. Something sinister was going on with Przemek ever since his arrest a few months ago.

Secrets? Leon jerks back, his head plunges into the pile of pillows behind him. You mean Zofia? He smiles spitefully. I can't wait for the kids to meet her.

You are not dying, so what's the rush?

Yeah, you would know, Leon clears his throat and stretches his arm towards a plastic cup with a straw by the bed. It's just beyond his reach. The newspaper slips off the bed and floats down to the floor. Jolanta grabs the cup and holds it for a few seconds, in front of his hand. His hair is not grey at all. He has bleached it! They both had laughed at an aging lothario in a grocery store, with frosted hair, a bottle of cheap wine and a frozen shrimp ring in his basket. Leon takes a few sips of water. His lips pucker around the straw like a cigarette.

Are we allowed to smoke here? Jolanta asks.

No, Leon says, I wish.

A loving family, Leon says and throws the empty cup towards the garbage can under the sink but misses. It's great to hear my wife and kids are so concerned about me. Just great. He stretches out the syllables as if she were too dumb to understand the irony.

Since my brush with death, I want to make some changes in my life, and so I want to talk to you. Leon puts his hands together, fingers interlaced.

Excellent, Jolanta smiles. I want to talk to you also. She opens her purse. Where did I put this...she mumbles.

But tell me first, my loving and devoted wife, why did it take you five fucking days to see me in the hospital after a coronary? Leon's spit flies out of his mouth and his tanned face gets sunburn red. They called you from the fucking ambulance! I could hear you on the phone! Veins twist and rope along his neck.

My God, relax Leon! Jolanta pushes him back down on the pillow. She can feel his chest spasm. God forbid he dies now from the second heart attack. Things would really get complicated. I told you, I came as soon as I could, she says. He moves his catheterized hand away. She pats the edge of the bed.

No, you said 'as soon as you heard.' They called you on Tuesday, not Wednesday, not Thursday, not Friday or Saturday. Five days Jolanta! I could be dead.

Yes I know. She takes out a tissue from the box on the bedside table and dabs her eyes. She feels like the tears are going to come any minute now. I thought you were dead when they called. I thought you left me all alone. That's why as soon as I heard I ran to the bank to close our account. Twisted my ankle in a pothole.

What? Your husband is dying and your first reaction is to take money out of our account? Wait a second, our joint account? I thought we took you off it, since you had your own. Leon's eyes flit around the room, as if he is searching for the panic button.

Well, we did...talk about it. And I thought we decided not to do that.

She finally found it in the bag, the small printout. It was wedged in the bottom, under the wallet and the spare key.

So I went there, in case you were dead, to get the money.

I am not dead, woman!

No, you definitely aren't. Neither are your finances.

What are you talking about? He rolls his eyes.

I get half, she says and stares at him. Or I take everything if you divorce me.

What?

When were you going to tell me you have fifty grand American dollars in your account! That's two hundred thousand *złoty*! She shoves the banknote under his nose. She has been holding it in her hand so tight it hurts, as if the balance would disappear, one digit after another, if she let go.

Oh my God! Leon whispers and rubs his scraggly face, the loose flesh rolling up and down.

Yeah, it's a miracle, really. Is that where you were all this time? A casino?

I gave Zofia the wrong account number. I think I'm gonna be sick. His face goes pale. He flaps his hand in the direction of a kidney-shaped basin next to the sink.

Jolanta jumps to her feet. The purse falls on the floor. The extra key slips out and skids deep under the bed.

Where did you get all this money? Jolanta hands him the pan.

He is taking big breaths. He rests the basin on his lap.

I sold mother's flat.

Didn't your brother and his wife buy it from the housing association years ago?

Leon smirks. They did, he says, but they put it in her name. They didn't want her to feel bad while she was still alive. But they are all the way in Canada, and I am here. And she always felt bad, you know...I'm the favourite son.

Wasn't it supposed to be theirs? Jolanta can't suppress a smile. She has always hated Magda, the Sunday church-goer, perfectly prepared Christmas and Easter meals, the Bible, the holy wafer on the table. That smug hausfrau with not a grain of sex appeal or intelligence. And her constant bragging about her genius children, that was the worst.

Why should Jarek and Magda have everything? Leon is on a roll. He wipes the spit off his lips with the back of his hand. They have an apartment in Toronto, their old flat in Warsaw, they just bought a new flat for Tomek in Krakow, and now this? And I am to have nothing? You should have seen their faces when they came back. They hadn't expected her to change her will! What did they think, leaving me to look after her alone to change her stinking diapers, spoon-feed her, while they live the good life in Canada? As soon as she went to the hospice, they were in her apartment, scrubbing the floors, emptying the closets, washing everything. As if it was theirs already. Saying how they wish she would get better and live another hundred years while we were all just waiting for her to die.

Hypocrites, Jolanta whispers. She clears her throat. So what are you going to do with all that money, Leon?

Well now, he rubs his hands. Buy stocks, play some cards, live a little?

Don't you need to buy a place to live? she asks, thinking of the new key.

Zofia has a place.

Zofia? She is going to throw you out as soon as she realizes who you are. She doesn't love you as I do.

Zofia put me on the deed. She is dying you know. Cancer. I am going to take care of her as I did mother.

Jolanta is stunned. She blinks slowly. He is still smiling.

So, she thinks, he is going to come back, eventually. You have it all planned I see, she says. But, I am no Zofia. You owe me. I kept us all afloat while you were too proud to look for a job. All these years, your head in the bottle, while I paid the kids' tutors, the school bribes, the bail. I would have taken it all, but for such a large sum they needed your signature.

What bail?

Yeah, while you were out romancing Zofia, Przemek got arrested for stealing. Lucky I have friends. All my savings. Something happened to him there. When is the last time you talked to him?

Oh, no, you are not going to blame it on me. I am not the one who took him out of school to sit in your fucking stall selling overpriced used clothing. You were never home! Mother cooked for us while you were out riding trains, doing who knows what. His fingers twist the edge of the blanket. The IV pump starts beeping.

I worked hard. For you, for them.

For money, he snaps.

I am not ashamed to say I love money. I love to haggle, I love thinking up ways to make more money. It makes me happy. It is so much better than sitting on my ass all day, drinking, feeling sorry for myself because no one wants to hire me, the big shot Mr. Architect, the wino. And your mommy always there to feed your ego, with her little jarred soups and preserves. As if I couldn't cook.

You never—

That doesn't mean I don't know how. I just won't. I am not some submissive little mouse who takes blame for everything. I want what's mine. Jolanta bends forward, her face inches away from Leon's. If I don't get half, I'm going to tell the kids about the money. They will pick your bones clean.

So that's how it is. He leans back, as if she is going to bite his face. He sighs. Give me a cigarette, he says. Open the window, would you?

She throws a pack of *Sobieski's* and a lighter in his lap and opens the window. The Palace of Culture and Science squats on the horizon like a dark pagan god.

I'll give you thirty percent, Leon says, taking a drag.

Forty-five, Jolanta reaches for the cigarette pack he is holding. He grabs her hand and squeezes until she gasps.

Forty, and you don't tell the kids, he says.

Deal, she says.

Leon lets go of her hand. I like your shirt, new? He blows smoke at her cleavage.

Jolanta lights a cigarette.

The door opens, and Zofia walks in, carrying dinner in a Styrofoam box. She sniffs at the air and forces a cough.

The key is under your bed, Jolanta says. On the way out she throws the cigarette butt out the window.

It's not too late, she has still time to go back to her stall and convince a few more people she has what they need.

ACKNOWLEDGMENTS

I would like to thank my husband Steffen for his continuing support and for making it possible to write full time. I am eternally grateful to my mother for Polish Romantic Era poetry and vivid storytelling; my father—for sharing his imagination. Big thanks my writing friends, Bob, Karen, Lisa, and Margaret, for editorial advice, encouragement, and support in all my writing and editing projects. I want to especially thank Denis De Klerck from Mansfield Press for making my childhood dream a reality, and Julie Booker who edited the stories before publication.

PUBLISHING CREDITS:

Lemons was published in the *Bristol Short Story Anthology Volume 9*, 2016

Bozia was published in *When the Door Opened: Poetry and Short Stories from the 2014 gritLIT Competition*.

Kasia Jaronczyk is a cell biologist by training. She has published poems and short stories in *Carousel, Room, The Prairie Journal, Carousel, Nashwaak Review*, and in *Postscripts to Darkness* (an anthology of dark & horror fiction). Her stories have won first place at the Eden Mills Writers' Festival Fiction Contest in 2010 and second place in the gritLIT festival in 2014. Her work was longlisted for the CBC Radio Literary Award 2010 and shortlisted for the Bristol Prize 2016. She is the co-editor of *Polish(ed): Poland Rooted in Canadian Fiction*, an anthology of Polish-Canadian and Polish-themed short stories forthcoming from Guernica Editions in September 2017.